THE OPPOSING VENUS

THE OPPOSING VENUS

THE COMPLETE CABALISTIC CASES OF
SEMI DUAL, THE OCCULT DETECTOR

J.U. GIESY AND
JUNIUS B. SMITH

ALTUS PRESS
2018

PUBLISHING HISTORY

"The Opposing Venus" originally appeared in the October 13, 20, 27, and November 3, 1923 issues of *Argosy* magazine (Vol. 155, Nos. 1–4). Copyright © 1923 by The Frank A. Munsey Company. Copyright renewed © 1950 and assigned to Steeger Properties, LLC. All rights reserved.

THANKS TO

W.J. Andrew Franklin & Janice Roberts

Visit *altuspress.com* for more books like this.

TABLE OF CONTENTS

THE RETURN OF SEMI DUAL

IT HAS BEEN said that there is nothing new under the sun, and especially in the realms of literature. This may be true, and if we go back to civilizations long perished from the memory of man—perhaps to that famed Atlantis, now lying at the bottom of the deep—we may find that it is true, indeed. But of literature, as we know it, it may be said without fear of successful contradiction, that the Semi Dual stories are an exception to that rule.

Away back in 1911, there came unheralded, addressed to the "Editor of Argosy," a script labeled "Semi Dual." The name showed it a title picked by amateurs, but the contents and their nature had never greeted editorial eyes before. Here was a story different—as different from every-day fiction as day is from night. It was purchased on the spot and given to the world in the early months of 1912 under the title of "The Occult Detector." But the name which the authors psychologically sensed as the one to endure, stuck in the minds of those who read, until Semi Dual became visualized to countless readers as more than an imaginary being.

Semi Dual—the joint creation of two minds, trained in medicine, science and law. Readers of the *Argosy*, the *All-Story*, the *Cavalier*, will recall his numerous appearances through the pages of those magazines, his solving of intricate problems and always by a dual solution—one material, for material minds—the other occult, for those who cared to sense a deeper some-

1

thing back of the philosophic lessons interwoven in the narrative of each story.

We know that the Semi Dual stories in the past created world-wide interest, for thousands of letters greeted their appearance and voiced demand for more. Who, of our old readers, will not recall such stories as "The Wisteria Scarf," "Rubies of Doom," "The House of the Ego," "The Ghost of a Name," to mention just a few of more than a score of these novels which have appeared. And scarcely need we mention "Black and White" and "Wolf of Erlik," to recall Semi Dual's more recent appearance on the covers of this magazine.

That these stories are the work of master craftsmen, cannot be denied. Always a story to tell from the beginning of their writing career, the creators of Semi Dual have improved in art and technique as the years went by. But art and technique alone could not have given to the world such stories as those twined about the character of Semi Dual.

J.U. Giesy is a physician and surgeon. Junius B. Smith is an attorney-at-law—yet we are told by these two gentlemen, that to acquire a worthwhile knowledge of Hermetic Philosophy and Astrology, more time is consumed and more persistent application is necessary than to learn medicine, surgery and law combined.

That their knowledge of the occult and the stars is profound, may be inferred from their election as Fellows of the American Academy of Astrologians—the highest honor that can come to any delver into Nature's hidden mysteries.

We are told by Messrs. Giesy and Smith that one does not really understand the meaning of life until he understands the soul and the science of the stars.

The world was turned topsy-turvy some time ago. People, by circumstance, were forced aside from their accustomed pursuits to business of immediate international importance. The stories of Semi Dual disappeared from the pages of this magazine. The pendulum of human emotions, however, is now again swinging toward the transcendental, gaining momentum with amazing suddenness. Giesy and Smith and the editors both feel that the time is ripe for a return of this famous character.

In "The Opposing Venus" you will find him in one of his best moods. Read it, tell us what you think of it, let us know whether we shall again place Semi Dual before you at regular intervals, as we did at your behest for so many years in the past. This magazine is run for you and what you want we will get, if humanly possible.

Tell us: Shall we have more of Semi Dual?

CHAPTER I

A CALL FOR HELP

"SAY—" DANNY QUINN, our red-headed office boy, whom my partner, James Bryce, had recruited from the ranks of the city newsies, announced as he followed his rap into my private den, where Jim and I were sitting, "I reckon that city tec Johnson must have got a line on somethin' too big for him to handle. Anyway, he's outside wantin' to know if he can horn in here. Shall I let him or throw him out?"

Danny was loyal to the interests of "Glace & Bryce—Private Investigators," but had small respect for the central office force, and being a protégé of Jim's he comported himself very much according to the dictates of the shrewd little brain he carried around beneath his brick-dust thatch.

I glanced at Bryce. Before we organized our firm, he himself had been a member of the city force. Johnson and he were friends. And as the former was no man to spend time on a merely social visit and had appealed to us for aid on more than one occasion, there was justification for Danny's supposition that if he were seeking an interview at present there was something in the wind.

Jim nodded.

"That will do, Dan," I said. "Show Inspector Johnson in."

Danny winked and withdrew, and a moment later Johnson opened the door.

He was a large man, rather heavy of figure, with brown hair and eyes and a ruddy tinge to his skin.

" 'Lo, boys. How's tricks?" he spoke in greeting as he helped himself to a chair and balanced his hat on his knees.

"Nothin' doing." Bryce told him the literal truth. "Gordon an' I was just wonderin' if th' preachers had finally convinced th' public that bustin' laws didn't pay."

John nodded. "Oh, well," he said, "I wouldn't worry. I don't guess they've put th' devil out of business. Course this private game you're sittin' into ain't much like the old days, Jim, but it ain't likely you're goin' to starve for a lack of a little human cussedness to keep you on th' job."

"That's encouragin'." Bryce eyed him, pursing out his stubby brown mustache. And suddenly he gave vent to a chuckle.

"What particular form of cussedness brought you up here? Come on—kick in, 'stead of sidlin' all around th' subject like a pup round a saucer of milk. What's on your mind?"

Johnson's lips twitched as he answered. "J.H. Dorien."

"The importer of oriental fabrics?" I asked as he paused to note, so I suspected, what effect his response produced upon us.

He ducked an affirmative head. "Yes. Know him?"

"I know *of* him," I replied. And I did. J.H. Dorien was the head of a considerable business and a somewhat lurid young man—a sport, a spender—one who went in for horses, motors, and women, particularly the last if common report was to be believed—a bachelor—reputedly wealthy. I asked another question:

"What's happened to J.H.?"

"He's been shot," said Johnson.

"Killed?" Bryce suggested, with quickened interest.

"Not yet." Johnson grinned.

Jim sighed. "Well, now that the prologue's been played off, let's get down to the main action. Just where do we come in?"

Johnson shifted his hat to the top of my desk and hitched his chair around. "That's what I come up for—to see whether you would or not. There's something darned funny about th' thing from start to finish. I thought maybe you'd like to take a hand."

"Yeh?" Bryce produced one of his deadly black cigars and bit off the end. "How d'ye mean, funny?"

"Why—Dorien was shot three times—once in th' head— once in the breast and once in the arm, and—he won't talk."

Jim nodded and struck a match. "Well— don't know if that's funny or not. If I was shot in the head, I'm not sure I'd be de-liverin' any Chautauqua lectures myself," he opined.

"Oh, you couldn't be shot in th' head." Once more Johnson grinned. "But—listen. Dorien can talk all right if he wants to—but he won't. He's making a noise like a clam."

Jim blew out smoke. "Then—where's it any skin off your back?" he inquired.

"Ordinarily it wouldn't be, of course. But so far as we know anything about it, it's a mighty raw bit of work. We've reason to believe that Dorien was the victim of a gang—"

"Black hand or blackmail?" Jim cut in.

"Blackmail," said Johnson shortly, "and it ain't their first piece of work by a long shot, but it is the first time there's been any shooting mixed up in the stuff they've pulled."

"Meanin'," Bryce made rather cynical comment, "they've sort of took off th' muffler an' made too much noise. Still I haven't seen anything about it in th' papers—"

"And you won't." Johnson's color heightened a trifle and he frowned. "I told you Dorien wasn't talking and it's his affair whether he puts up a holler or not. That's a hot line of chatter you're using. You know as well as I do that it ain't th' depart-ment's place to wet-nurse the public.

"We can't chaperon a lot of darned fools that go lookin' for trouble, an' find it through mixin' themselves up in some sort of a rotten mess. An' if they choose to get themselves out again th' best way they can an' pay th' piper, it ain't our part to butt in unless they file a complaint. That's about what's been goin' on in this burg for some considerable time. Dorien ain't th' first by a long shot, but up to now nobody's hollered for help."

"An', accordin' to your own say-so," Bryce reminded, "Dorien ain't exactly screamin'. An' if he ain't, I reckon there's a reason an' I reckon it wears skirts."

"You're a darned good guesser," said our guest. "There's always a skirt mixed up in this mob's work."

"Know her?"

"Know her?" The inspector took a deep breath. "Of course we know her. She's Roma Temple. That much is easy. She was with Dorien at the time he was shot."

"The girl was?" I interjected.

"Yes."

"And where did the shooting occur?"

"In Dorien's rooms over here in the Monks Hall." Johnson mentioned a very modern and ornate apartment erected a couple of years before on Park Drive, in the most exclusive part of the city. "He's got a mighty swell dump over there, and I reckon they must have had a slip up somewhere. Anyway, Dorien was shot and somebody called a cab and carted him over to a hospital and left him. Oh, they tried to hush the matter up."

"And where is the Temple girl now?"

Johnson eyed me. "She's down at the Kenton as big as you please. Got a suite there, and a woman companion—chaperon, I suppose you'd call her, name of Mrs. Meese. She's supposed to be a Western heiress, or somethin' of that sort, accordin' to what I can gather—"

"Say," Bryce broke in, "what was this—a fancy sort of badger game, or what?"

"I wouldn't wonder," said Johnson. "It looks a good deal like it on its face. This mob we think the girl belongs to have been specializin' on stuff more or less like that for th' past two years. They get their fall guy mixed up with some jane and then they put on the screws. It's about time it was stopped."

"Migosh," Bryce grinned. "You've answered my question at last. This run-in gives you a first class chance. You've got about three definite charges at least—unlawful possession of firearms, assault with intent to kill, attempted extortion."

"Sure," Johnson nodded. "We have if we can find anybody to hang 'em on to. So far we haven't. I've told you th' thing's been hushed up an' Dorien won't talk."

"You've seen him?" I questioned.

"Oh, yes, I've seen him," he returned in a tone of disgust. "It was like this. The patrolman on that beat reported. He saw Dorien carried out and put into the cab, and made a note of its number, an' he saw a drop or two of blood on the curb after the thing had left. We ran down the driver an' the fellow told us he'd took a man to th' hospital, pretty badly shot up.

"It was easy enough to find Dorien after that, and to run out quite a lot besides. But the minute we struck th' man himself we hit a snag. About all he had to say was that he wasn't asking any help from the department, and until he did, he'd thank us to keep out."

"He's still at the hospital?" I asked.

"No. He's back home. This thing happened about a month ago. He's getting over it, but is sort of weak."

"Then what's the notion?" said Bryce.

"Th' notion is that if we can get a line on what really happened, we're goin' to bust up this outfit," Johnson rasped. "Look at it, you two. I'm a bull—an' I've been one most of my life, an' I ain't got many illusions left, an' I know what they say about th' department, but—it makes me sick.

"Here's a mob organized to just naturally capitalize human dirt—usin' a bunch of women to work on th' natural damn foolishness of men, an' then bleed 'em. No wonder th' suckers won't talk. An' it wouldn't matter so much if it was only them an' th' women this bunch is usin', but it ain't. Some of these men are married. There's good women mixed up in this rottenness—or at least affected by it, an'—kids, all for a few dirty dollars."

I nodded. All at once Johnson was talking from the heart. Sincerity rang in his voice. And I knew him, had known him for years—that he was a man absolutely honest, absolutely loyal to the functions of his office.

"But if Dorien won't talk, and the whole thing's been hushed up, why do you think this affair was the work of that sort of a gang?" I asked.

His eyes lighted. "Because—Roma Temple is known to be pretty thick with a guy by th' name of Archer Kell, or 'Kelley' as they call him—an' we've a pretty straight hunch that he's th' head of that kind of mob. He does nothing, always has money, is a swell dresser—oh, you boys know the type—th' sort that are apt to live off women one way or another."

"Then," I said, "it boils down to this: you think Dorien was shot as the result of a frame-up in which the Temple girl played a part—"

"A big one," Johnson interrupted. "She was the bait"

"All right," I accepted. "But you can't find out who fired the shots. How about this Archer Kell or Kelley?"

Johnson frowned. "I thought of that, but—he's about town same as ever."

"All right," I said again. "Now, in what way can we help?" Even then I had a suspicion of his answer, and he proved me instantly right.

"Why—I'm tryin' to find out somethin' there don't seem any way of learnin' so far as I've gone, an' I don't know of but one man alive who can pull that sort of trick."

Semi Dual! Bryce's and my strange friend who lived on the roof of the Urania building where we had our office suite. From this unusual abode, which he had constructed for himself, with its garden full of growing things, roofed over by curving plates of green yellow glass against the sting of winter, and sumptuous quarters in the tower of the Urania, set like a pure white temple in the center of the garden, a little private telephone line led down to a box on the wall of the room wherein we sat. Semi Dual—the modern student of nature's higher forces—a reader of the stars—a believer in the law of retributive justice, which measures to each man according to his actions, so that in very truth indeed he reaps in time a harvest partaking in its nature of the thing he sows—the law of cause and effect, which in its widest application holds each man responsible in the creative scheme for his every thought and act and word.

To him astrology, telepathy, psychometry, and other of the so-called occult subjects of research, at which mankind in the mass is apt to scoff or regard from a merely superstitious viewpoint, were open books. I myself had been a doubting Thomas when first I met him, but later I became convinced—came to accept his teachings that all force is one—and matter but its expression in a concrete way, be that matter involved in man, or a living germ or the rocks or the trees. And when one looks at things that way it explains a great deal.

It had been Semi Dual who had originally led Bryce and me to organize our firm. He stood to us very much as the god from the machine. Time after time he had bent his unusual faculties to our need in unraveling some intricate tangle on which we were engaged.

And with all his powers of knowing the unknowable—or what seemed the unknowable from every-day standards—Dual was a practical man. He was neither charlatan nor dreamer. He knew life values—the limits of human credence. And knowing it, he never sought to strain it.

"Material proof for material man, Gordon my friend," he had said to me many times when seeking to support some of his own deductions by means of palpable evidence.

Johnson knew him—had even worked with him more than once in the running down of a crime. And though he admitted that Semi left him baffled, I think that deep in his soul his faith in Dual's ability was little more than a degree behind Jim's and mine. Hence his coming thus to enlist Semi's aid through us, when he found himself once more faced by a perplexing problem, could hardly be considered strange.

I heard Bryce draw in his breath as Johnson spoke, and then he voiced a comment. "I reckon Dual could find the jasper you're after if anybody could, but—th' question is—would he be willin' to take it on?"

For Semi was a man to whom mere petty crime—the theft of a jewel or a sum of money meant nothing—to whom the objects for which mundane man is always striving were but passing things. To him the soul—the spiritual values—were the only really worth while issues in the cosmic scheme. And because of that I answered before Johnson made any comment:

"I've an idea that he would, not because of any injury to Dorien short of death, or any sum of which he may have been mulcted, provided there was any loss, but because, as Johnson says, his major object is to put an end to the operations of this gang—that would appear to be prostituting women and de-bauching men for the purpose of gaining a certain filthy wealth. I think that is the angle of this affair on which he might very probably consent to take it up."

"That's th' talk," said Johnson. "Dorien ain't a white lamb to be protected, but it makes me hot to see this bunch gettin' away with these plays year after year."

Bryce nodded. "Well, if you think Semi would be willin' I don't see why we shouldn't buy a stack or two in th' game, do you?"

"No," I said, "I don't. And we can soon settle the first point."

I rose and turned toward the little telephone box on the wall. It was in my mind to call Dual and ask him if we could let Johnson explain the situation.

But before I reached it, its buzzer whirred, with a staccato suddenness that actually made me pause, and both Jim and Johnson sat bolt upright.

CHAPTER II

THE SEER OF THE TOWER

I THREW THEM a glance. They sat there, eyes involuntarily widened, bodies frozen into a rigid attention, and I laughed.

Remember what I have said about Semi Dual's belief that all force is one, his use of telepathy among other so-called occult things. For if force is actually universal, then the product of mental activity which we denominate thought, is as much a thing as the wireless currents shot forth from the antennae of a tower along the Hertzian waves. Personally I knew Dual possessed the ability of sensing such lines of force and translating them into meaning. And here we three had been sitting, discussing Johnson's problem for the past hour, while all the time his brain at least had been centered on the major purpose of his visit. Wherefore Dual had caught the mental vibration. He had done such things within my knowledge before.

Anyway, I put it to the proof. I removed the receiver and answered what could only be his call:

"Glace speaking."

His voice came back to me, low pitched, deep, full, calm with the matter of factness of a merely casual suggestion:

"If Inspector Johnson wishes to consult with me, Gordon, suppose you bring him up."

"Thanks," I accepted, "I will." I hung up, turned around and repeated Semi's invitation.

Jim grinned.

Johnson put up a heavy hand and ran a finger about his neck inside his collar. He got up.

"Every time he does a thing like that, it gets me, but"—he reached for his hat—"it's what I wanted when I came here. Let's go."

We went out and caught an up-going cage, to leave it on the twentieth floor and mount bronze and marble stairs. It was the approach to Semi's domain upon the roof. There was an inlaid plate of glass and metal at the top let into a pathway that led from the stairs to the tower between beds of flowers and shrubs. One trod upon it and rang a chime of bells in the tower to announce his coming.

As they pealed out, soft, mellow as temple bells in some shrine of a half-forgotten god, Johnson paused and jerked a hand at the vine-covered parapet walls about the garden.

"An' out there," he said, "is th' world th' way we know it, an' here's—this. I ain't emotional as a rule, but every time I come here I can't help feelin' it's different—as if there was somethin' here th' rest of us are missin', even if I can't put a name to th' thing myself. I've felt th' same way once or twice when I got out in th' hills with just th' clouds an' th' trees."

That was quite a rhapsody for him and I assented to his mood. "What the everyday world is missing is peace."

"Peace?" he echoed almost sharply.

"Yes—a harmony of thought and action." For always it had seemed to me that the very spirit of peace and harmony was brooding here upon this roof.

"Well—I don't know but you're right," he said as we went on along the path.

We reached the tower. Its door was opened by Henri, Dual's constant and only companion, who ushered us into a room done in soft, deep browns, and across it to a farther door, which he swung wide before us.

We filed through it and into the presence of Semi Dual.

He lifted warm gray eyes at our coming. As was his habit

here in his own abode, he was clad in long loose robes of white, edged on cuff and skirt with purple.

"Be seated, my friends," he said with a smile that lingered on his strong-lipped mouth while we helped ourselves to chairs. "And now, inspector, in what way may I hope to prove of assistance?"

I saw Johnson's eyes as always when he came here run about the room, with its priceless Persian rug, its great and ancient clock in the corner, its bronze and life-sized figure of Venus bearing the golden apple, which was no more than an electrolier at one end of the massive desk beside which Dual was sitting. And then he plunged into the story of Dorien's shooting much as he had given it to Jim and myself, except that now he told it straight through from start to finish, since in all the time of its narration, Semi did not interrupt.

Instead, he lay back in his chair and closed his eyes. Save for the rise and fall of his deep, full chest, he did not move until Johnson came to a close. Then and then only he sat erect and asked a second question:

"And what, Mr. Johnson, is your purpose in all this?"

"Why—I want to bust this gang wide open." Johnson drew an actually rasping breath. "Why—look at it, Mr. Dual. Why—if I've got my dope right, they're taking girls an' trainin' 'em to th' job—educatin', you understand, to trap men. It's a pretty filthy business, an' I thought—"

"Ah, yes," said Semi Dual, and for just an instant I saw a spark of what seemed leaping light, flash deep in the clear gray of his eyes, "it is a filthy business indeed—a perversion of what should be held sacred—a fouling of the fount of life itself—for behold, Mr. Johnson, and you my other friends as well, a great truth: The Life of Man is a pure stream which flows through the bodies of men and women unsullied unless mayhap it be clouded by those individual actions which mankind denominates sin, wherein Woman becomes the Temple of Life and Man the High Priest—and whosoever save the High Priest shall enter the Holy of Holies which lies within the Temple, or rend the Veil before it—that one profanes a shrine. These things are set down in the Kabbala of the Hebrews for those who understand. And whoso breaks the law, by the law shall that one be broken. At what time was Dorien shot?"

"Ten o'clock on the mornin' of May 15th, as near as we can place it," Johnson told him.

I glanced at Bryce. He was pursing out his stubby brown mustache. Semi's words had been characteristic, and what I saw in Jim's face indicated plainly that, like myself, he was convinced that Johnson had won the ally he sought.

Nobody spoke, however, as Semi noted the time of the shooting on a bit of paper, and it was his voice broke the silence:

"And—have you any knowledge of his birth date?"

"Why, no," Johnson said, "but I reckon I could dig it up at th' Bureau of Vital Statistics. You know they've got a record of all th' births that are reported—"

"Exactly," Dual accepted. "Do so. I believe there is a space for the birth time on the official blanks. And some physicians are in the habit of noting the hour of birth by watch time at least. If you know the woman, describe her physical appearance."

"She ain't a bad looker. About twenty-four or five, I'd say, and a swell dresser," Johnson began. "She's rather short, with a good figure, blond hair and complexion, and well-shaped features, an' from all I can gather, she's mighty attractive to men. Of course, she'd have to be to get away with the sort of work the mob I think she's hooked up with is pullin'."

Dual nodded. "Possibly a Neptune type," he said half to himself.

"Eh? I don't get you?" Johnson eyed him.

"No, Mr. Johnson." Semi put out a hand and drew to him a sheet of paper on the desk. Lifting a pair of calipers, he spun a circle upon it, cut it into twelve parts, set down a numeral counterclockwise opposite each dividing line, before he continued, smiling: "Give me an hour, my friends. Pass it in my garden or devote it to your own affairs. Return to me at its end."

I got up, and so did Jim and Johnson. Personally I knew what Dual was doing—that his intervention in the human problem Johnson had brought to him had begun—that he was about to erect an astrological figure based on the time of Dorien's shooting—a horary chart so called—and that after we had gone out of this room where he sat and spun his circle on a virgin sheet of paper, he would write down upon it other symbols and signs, such as he used in those computations of his wherein he sought to read the influence of the stars themselves upon mortal mundane affairs.

I led the way out and Jim and the inspector followed without a word. When we stood in the sunlight of the garden, Jim spoke. "Well—I guess you got what you come for. An' seein' as we've got to kill an hour, we might as well do it here. Come over an' sit down an' rest your heels. I've got a question or two I'd like to ask myself."

He led the way to a seat beside a little fountain where ruddy goldfish were floating among budded lily pads.

Johnson sat down and once more ran a finger about his collar while Jim and I found seats and Bryce lighted another cigar. "Yes," he agreed, "I reckon I've got what I come for. He's sittin' in there now drawin' them figures of his on a piece of paper, addin' 'em up, dividin' 'em, multiplyin' 'em, takin' their square root for all I know, to find out how a man come to be shot. On th' level—I've knowed him to do it often, but every time it gets my goat. It's—it's sort as if he knew so danged much more than I do, that he'd worked out a regular mathematics of life."

A mathematics of life. My brain caught at his words. After all I found myself thinking, it wasn't a bad definition—was a fairly good, if not too comprehensive, definition of what Dual was employing toward the end of knowledge, back there in the tower where he sat in his white and purple robes. A mathematics of life, which showed how and why man the puppet did this thing or that, to the pull of invisible strings, the urge of invisible cosmic forces as the cosmos moved.

"An'," Johnson ran along, "he always makes me feel as if he was sayin' two things at once. He says this Temple skirt is a Neptune type, an' while I ain't exactly certain, as I recall it, Neptune was a god of th' fishes or somethin' like that among th' ancient Greeks."

Bryce cleared his throat. "Which ain't th' reason why I brought you over here beside the fishes. It's a nice place to sit. Maybe he meant she was one of Neptune's daughters. Neptune's a star, ain't he, Glace?"

I nodded.

"Well, then," said Jim, "that point being settled, th' next one is, who's this Archer Kell or Kelley?"

Johnson scowled. "He's an educated crook. That's what he is. I've told you about how he works. He gets a line on some rich guy and frames a deal by which he can get him into his clutches, sets one of these women he uses to trap him and makes his shakedown, after she's done her part. He's a sort of moral con man, an' lives on his wits. Good lookin' enough unless you look too close. Then you can see th' devil in his face. He's simply a wrong un, Jim, from start to finish, though I reckon he must have come of good people once. Light brown hair, blue gray eyes, high cheek bones, 'bout five feet eight to eight an' a half in height, dresses like a gentleman or a lounge lizard if you know what I mean—men's clothes till around six an' a hammertail or a dinner coat after that."

"And," I said, "you're sure he's been in town since the shooting?"

"Yep." Johnson turned to me. "I am, because I made it a point to find out. He's been laid up in his rooms with a busted arm for th' best part of a month an' is just beginnin' to get about."

"Busted?" Jim repeated sharply.

"Yes. Between th' elbow an' shoulder. Just got it out of a cast. Right arm," Johnson vouched additional information.

I looked at Bryce. His eyes were narrowed. "Him an' Dorien both," he remarked. "They must have had a lovely rough house."

"Oh, hold on!" Johnson shrugged. "I ain't sayin' Kelley shot him. Th' main thing about him is that I've a notion Roma Temple is a member of his mob."

"An' they was after Dorien's check book."

"Sure. Their play is to keep still an' let th' money talk."

"I suppose Dorien has a man in that place of his?" Jim suggested.

Johnson nodded. "Jap."

"An' th' girl—has she gone to see either of these guys since Dorien was shot up?"

"Oh, yes," said Johnson, sneering. "She's gone to see 'em—both."

"But great cat!" Jim exploded. "D'ye think they ain't done with Dorien—yet? If they framed him an' he knew it, she'd hardly be goin' to see him. Look here, I reckon she could know both him an' Kelley without belongin' to any mob. You said she's supposed to be a Western heiress at th' Kenton, an' she's got a chaperon an' all that. Is it dead sure this Kelley ain't campin' on her trail himself if she's rich?"

Johnson gave him a pitying glance. "I've always said you was a clever cuss," he remarked with a chuckle. "Th' only trouble with your latest demonstration is that, I also told you, I had plenty of cause to think she'd helped Kelley with more than one deal of a similar nature before this."

"Then—" Bryce's tone grew almost pugnacious.

"Just that," said Johnson, grinning. "One guess is as good as another. That's why I came here."

"Time's up," I prompted, looking at my watch.

We went back to the tower, across the outer room to the farther door and rapped.

"Come," Dual's voice bade us enter.

He sat as we had left him, save that now there were several

sheets of paper, covered with the symbols of his calculations before him on the desk.

"Mr. Johnson," he spoke in a tone that betrayed a fully awakened interest, "this seems on its face a somewhat peculiar matter—somewhat contradictory, decidedly involved. My calculations, based on the time of the shooting, reveal one of the most interesting problems I have recently met. In the figure of the actual shooting, there appears what seems a cross purpose— a warfare of opposing forces—a certain indication of injury, thwarted, thrust aside from a fatal termination, by an influence cast from an unexpected source.

"Venus, which is Miss Temple's significator in my estimation, is exceedingly weak at the time of the shooting, and yet I am of the opinion that while it was directly because of her that Dorien, to which I assign Jupiter in my interpretation of this figure, was shot, yet she was actually largely responsible, due to her temporary position in saving him from death."

"Venus was?" Johnson frowned. "You mean Miss Temple? Well, that's like a woman. They're always raising the devil and then claiming they didn't mean to. But—I thought you said something about her an' Neptune before we went outside."

Semi Dual smiled. None knew better than he that what he had said was literally Greek to Johnson. "Neptune," he returned, "becomes here the octave expression of Venus. I said the woman was of a Neptune type. That being the case, it would not be surprising if the man should see the best in her nature and take her into his house."

"Sure," Johnson said, "she was there when he was shot. But— hittin' from th' shoulder, Mr. Dual, I don't know what you're talking about."

"It is not to be expected that you should," Dual replied. "But briefly, in such a figure as I have set up, each planetary symbol is allotted to some actor in the events known to have occurred. At ten o'clock on the day of the shooting, which, by the way, would appear to be very close to the actual time since the position of the planets at that hour would have predicated some such event, the indications are that Dorien would be injured so severely that he would barely escape death—that a woman would be the cause of whatever happened, that the entire affair would be the outcome of a plot—that there would have been dissension within the ranks of the plotters—that a secret enemy once more the woman, would in the course of past events have come to assume the aspect of a friend—that a sum of money or equivalent values would be a point of issue—that besides Dorien and the woman, I would say at least three men would be involved, one of them indicated by Uranus and one by Saturn, joint rulers of what is known as the seventh house in the figure I have set up—but that despite all that has gone before, Uranus being in Jupiter's own house, loses some of his oppositional sting, and Jupiter being in conjunction with the moon, and the sun coming to a favorable aspect, known as sextile, of the ascendant, we may assume that Dorien's life will be saved as we know it was."

And now Johnson nodded. "An' if that ain't a pretty good outline of a blackmailing scheme, I don't know what is," he declared in a tone of positive satisfaction. "An' that's just about how I'd doped it out. One of the three men might be this Archer Kell, I guess. Well—what have you got to suggest?"

"Two things," Dual returned. "First, that you get me Dorien's birth date without delay. Secondly, that I shall get in touch with Miss Temple in person. To the latter end—would it be possible, Mr. Johnson, for you to induce the management of the Kenton hotel to employ another bell boy, who might quite readily make the woman's acquaintance?"

"Why—I reckon I could fix it." Johnson narrowed his eyes.

Dual inclined his head. "Then—if you will do so—and if you, my two friends"—his glance turned to Jim and me—"will lend me your office boy for the endeavor—"

"Th' young sleuth!" Bryce erupted. "Well—by golly—he could

turn th' trick. Leave it to that red-headed kid to put it over. Just what's the notion?"

"Women," said Semi Dual, "particularly women engaging in a walk of life more or less outside the law, are apt to be superstitious. If when you go down, you will tell Danny I wish to see him, I will explain his duties to him and instruct him to report to Inspector Johnson as soon as he telephones you that his end of the matter is arranged. At that time he may also telephone you the date and hour of Dorien's birth. It is my intent that the boy shall lead this woman to me, of course. That is all for the present."

We rose and filed out. We left the roof and waited for a cage. Jim and I got out on our office floor and Johnson went on down. We called Danny into my private room and told him that Semi wanted to see him, and watched him depart.

And then and then only Jim voiced a grinning comment: "Darned if this ain't enough to make a man feel like quoting the Scriptures."

"Yes," I said, not exactly understanding.

He nodded with a chuckle. "Yep—'A little child shall lead 'em'—an' he's usin' that cherub of ours to lead th' Temple girl to him. That's how he works it. Can you beat it? Gosh!"

CHAPTER III

A PLAN OF ACTION

"**YES, IT'S THE** way he works," I agreed.

And it was. In all the time I had known him, it had always seemed that Semi Dual employed his unfailing knowledge of psychology toward the bringing about of his ends, as much as any other thing. And now that he was faced by Johnson's problem, about to undertake an intervention warranted only, as it appeared on the surface, by the inspector's desire to break up a band engaged in a sordid mulcting of men, by means of their own pitiful human weakness—now that he felt it needful to come into contact with a woman, an adventuress almost surely—one trained to watch carefully her every move, how better might he accomplish it than by setting Danny to the task. Surely even Roma Temple would be less apt to suspect a bell boy even if a new one in the hotel where she had her suite. I said as much to Jim, and once more he nodded.

"Oh, I'm wise to th' play, m'son, an' as for Dan, he's got red hair and so has a fox." He drew his watch and scanned it. "We might as well get our lunch."

We were back at the end of an hour to find Danny in his accustomed place, but with what struck me as a somewhat intent look on his freckled features.

He waited until we had gained my own den and then he rapped and came inside, making sure the door was closed behind him.

"I guess you know what's up," he began as he faced us.

"I understand that you're going to take a job at the Kenton as a bell hop," I said.

For a moment he made no answer and then: "Aw—quit kiddin', Mr. Glace. I gotta go down there an' close herd a chicken an' shoo her up here on th' roof. An' I'm to report to you if anything turns up. They're goin' to fix it so as to have th' room next hers left empty. I'm to tell Johnson to do that, an' to have her telephone fixed so th' hook stays up even when th' receiver's on it. They can do that with a bit of wire, Mr. Dual says, an' they can cut in a wire so's it will make a circuit with th' phone in th' other room. All I'll have to do will be to sit there with th' receiver to my ear, an' it will work as well as a dictograph. Gee— that man knows pretty near anything worth knowin'. I'll say he does. I'll bet that's a new one on Johnson."

I looked at Bryce. The thing was clever, I had to admit, and I did not doubt that if Dual said so, it would work. It was only another illustration of his infinite store of knowledge.

Jim met my regard and spoke to Danny. "That's all right, son. But before you go down there, get this. This thing's big, an' you've been given a pretty important part to play."

And Danny sobered. "I'm wise to that. Mr. Dual says he thinks this girl's in some sort of trouble, an' I can help him to help her if I manage to get her up to see him."

I glanced at Bryce again. Here, as I thought, was more psychology—a priming of Dan to a sympathetic attitude, by which Roma Temple might be best approached.

The telephone on my desk whirred.

I answered. It was Johnson calling to say everything was ready and to give me the date of Dorien's birth. He had certainly lost no time since he left us. I hung up, and told Dan to report to him at headquarters at once.

"On th' job," he said, his young eyes lighting with an avid interest. "I'll go down there an' try to help that 'bull' out. S'-long, Mr. Glace. S'-long, Mr. Bryce. You kin watch for my reports."

He departed with something of a swagger, and Bryce gave

vent to a chuckle. "A little child shall lead 'em, an' there's that telephone thing. Dan says it's a new one on Johnson, an' I ain't above admittin' it's a new one on me myself. But—it's slick. That way if any of th bunch happen to call on Roma, he can listen in on anything that's said."

I nodded and called Dual, telling him Danny was on his way to meet Johnson and giving him Dorien's day and hour of birth.

He repeated the latter as he wrote it down and added: "By this evening I shall hope to be ready with a suggestion of the first steps you shall take in this work."

It was that latter statement that took Bryce and me to the roof again that night and across it to that inner room in the tower where now the glowing apple in the hands of Venus threw a golden light across the paper-littered desk and etched in light and shadow the calm, strong features of our strange friend's face.

It shone, too, on a tray supporting a glass, a pitcher of silver and a plate containing one or two flat, round cakes of what I knew to be a sweetened paste. It came over me that he had eaten as he sat there—that from the time when we had left him until now, he had worked.

He glanced up as we entered and motioned us to chairs.

Jim produced a cigar and prepared to light it.

At the flare of the match, Semi pushed aside his papers and began to speak. "Verily, my friends, is it said that a man's fate is written from the hour of his birth cry, save that he lift up the eyes of his spirit and fix them on a distant goal like to a traveler in the darkness on a light. And man in his egotistical blindness, defies the lightnings and, Ajaxlike, draws down his doom upon himself. But what man knows when or where, or on whom the lightning shall fall, save that his fate shall overtake him, when the course of his self-sufficient groping is run out?"

"Still," said Jim, "there used to be quite a fad when I was a kid, of selling lightning rods. However, I reckon you're meanin' that this Dorien party had been sort of hunting trouble an' got it when the time was ripe."

"Within certain limits, Mr. Bryce. The chart I have set up for his birth, is a very interesting figure. In it Venus on the cusp of the ascendant is in direct opposition to Neptune."

"Oh, Venus," Jim interrupted. "A sort of opposing Venus. But I reckon that's womanlike. And from what you said to Johnson earlier to-day, it would look as though th' lady was rather opposing herself."

Dual's lips twitched slightly. "Many a man or woman has found himself in a similar condition, Mr. Bryce. Had Dorien been more prone to oppose his baser nature in the past, he would have found within him qualities which would have conspired to give him aid. But—he has 'lived his atoms,' as the saying is, and followed out their natal polarization as shown in his radical figure from which I would deem him to be a man of large-boned frame above medium height, with probably brown hair, eyes of a possible hazel and endowed with a fascinating quality apt to prove well-nigh irresistible to the opposite sex. For the rest his features should be large and well-shaped, partaking therein of the Jupiterian quality, but modified by the Venusian influence existing at his birth, which would naturally give a somewhat feminine cast to his nature, and at times perhaps to his voice.

"As a matter of fact, I should judge the man to be a combination of opposites from first to last. He is apt to make money, but spend it freely or actually lose it, although he is of good executive ability none the less. He is generous, bold, possessed of a strong will and a good self-control when he chooses to exercise it, and is close-mouthed concerning anything he does not wish to reveal.

"In some things he is stubborn to a degree, well-nigh unfeeling, prone to have his own way regardless of any consequence entailed. There is a warfare between his higher and lower love forces, wherein any woman of unconventional views or actions, such as are conducive to a debasing of mutual relations, is apt to have a strong effect upon him. Hence, he is apt to meet trouble in love and squandor money on women, and travel with what is commonly called the 'sporting' class. He is versatile, witty, courteous, refined in his creature tastes and in that the Venusian element of his nature once more shows. He may be sarcastic of tongue, at times a clever liar. He is threatened by martial accidents and injuries and misfortune come suddenly upon him.

"And the fact that the Moon, lady of the eighth house, or house of death, in his radical figure, is embraced by conjunction with Saturn, but separating from it, and that Mars casts a sextile to the Sun, while opposing the Moon and Saturn, and Saturn is in trine aspect to the Sun, brings us back to the subject of the shooting, indicating as it does that Dorien will nearly die, but not quite."

"Which is exactly what happened," I made comment as he paused.

"And as for his being close-mouthed, Johnson's already confirmed that, I reckon," said Bryce.

"Quite so," Dual assented. "Because of that we may assume that the man is keeping quiet merely because he does not wish to speak. Let us look again at the chart. The opposing Venus, as you have not inaptly called her, since throughout the matter within herself and her octave expression she appears to be swept into contradictory currents, is a woman of the Neptune type. Such a woman, particularly, would be very likely to have a pronounced effect on a man of Dorien's nature, and to be very strongly affected by him herself."

"But—" Jim stared. "You don't mean she'd be apt to fall in love with th' man she was set to bilk, by any possible chance."

Dual smiled. "Wheels within wheels, Mr. Bryce, and who can say where their course shall be run. Recall that I told Inspector Johnson that the man would be prone to see the best in the woman, and take her into his house."

In a way the speech was cryptic, but Jim did not hesitate. "You mean Dorien might have fallen for her hard enough to— protect her?"

"At least," said Semi, still smiling, "it would explain his announced determination not to talk."

"Holy smoke!" Jim snorted. "I guess Opposing Venus is right. If those two are sweet on each other, she's mighty apt right now to be in what you'd call opposition to this here Kelley and her mob."

I felt my attention quicken. "Look here," I said, "you told Dan that girl was in trouble."

His gray eyes met mine calmly. "And is not that one in trouble, Gordon, who is at war within himself? May not Roma Temple, the pawn in a sordid game, have come to a point where she sees at length with what utter ruthlessness the pawn is sometimes sacrificed?"

"But—the woman's an adventuress," I began.

"I said Dorien might see the best within her." His eyes still held me with an unwavering regard. "All force is one—and good and evil are terms of comparative quality only, and up and down are but mutual measures of distance as hot and cold are mutual measures of heat. As the atom in the cosmos vibrates, so its quality is determined, and life, my friend, is vibration, as vibration is the cosmic expression of force. Man's place on the scale depends then on the ratio of his vibration."

I gave it up. He always had an answer. And now it seemed to me that I caught a hint even if nothing more than a hint of some as yet unexpressed purpose in his words, something connected with Roma Temple herself. He had told Dan he could help her if he could bring her to him, and now he spoke of one at war within himself.

"And what is it you promised this afternoon to suggest as a first step on our part?" I asked.

"That you see Dorien sometime tomorrow," he made answer.

"See Dorien?" I repeated.

He inclined his head. "Perchance you may surprise him into some admission that shall prove of worth."

"But—he won't talk," Bryce proclaimed in a tone of complaint. Just what he had expected Dual to recommend, I don't know, but I do know that what he had suggested gave me a feeling of disappointment, and I thought I read a similar emotion in the expression of Jim's face. Trying to make Dorien divulge what he palpably meant to keep to himself appeared to me right then in the light of present conditions as a sort of labor of Tantalus.

Semi, however, met the objection once more, smiling.

"All men talk at times, my friend," he said. "And a straw may serve to show which way the wind blows, or to break a camel's back."

CHAPTER IV

SOME WORDS WITH DORIEN

BRYCE VOICED A suggestion of his own the next day before we essayed the task to which we had been set:

"Look here, m'son, I've been thinkin' an' I've doped it out like this: Johnson's already tried to make this bird loosen up an' scored a blank, an' Semi's put it up to us, an' I reckon th' only way we got a chance is to blow him up. We'll go over there an' pass ourselves off as private investigators, and spill enough of what we don't know exactly to get his attention at least. If Kelley and his mob really tried to frame him with the Temple girl as bait, an' we work it right, we may even get him into th' notion that we're part of the mob ourselves, an' if by any chance he's really sweet on th' girl like Dual hinted last night, an' we spill a few uncomplimentary remarks in her direction—"

"I get you," I interrupted. And it actually appeared to me as though his idea had as good a chance of netting us results as any other. Furthermore, Jim having been a policeman, he should certainly know how to grill his man to the best advantage. "We go over and—treat him rough."

"Well—yes," he assented slowly. "Not too rough, but—just rough enough. If we can get him hot under the collar—"

"He may boil over?"

Jim nodded. "Yes."

"Well—let's go and try it, anyway," I said, and rose.

We went down and caught a car that would take us close to the vicinity of Monks Hall. It was nearly two o'clock. We had purposely delayed our call till the afternoon, and it was almost half past two when we arrived before the ornate front of the apartment building and went in.

There was a hallway flanked by half pillars of artificial marble, a tiled floor, a gilded elevator grill, some potted palms, a telephone switchboard, and a combination telephone attendant and elevator operator on guard. He was a youth with a far from innocent countenance lighted by sophisticated eyes.

To him I gave our card, and explained that we would like to speak to Mr. Dorien in person, if we could.

"I don't know," he returned in a tone of consideration. "He ain't receivin' many callers right now. Been sick, but if you know him, maybe you know that already."

The remark was casual enough, but I suspected it was prompted by his perusal of the bit of pasteboard in his fingers. The thought shaped my reply.

"If you allude to what happened here the morning of May 15, we do. Suppose you call him up. And in order to make your announcement what it should be—here."

I extended a bill, and he took it, grinning. "Thanks."

He stepped to the switchboard and plugged a connection. "Mr. Dorien—this is Ed. Say—Mr. Dorien, there's a coupla men down here askin' for you, an' they won't take no for an answer." His voice sank to a lowered pitch. "Bulls or sumpin'. I gotta bring 'em up." He broke the connection and came back with a wink. "All right, sir, if you'll step into the cage."

We stepped. He followed and shot us aloft. Presently he brought the cage to a stop. "Third door to your right," he said, and slid back the door.

A woman, not over five feet two, with a figure gracefully turned despite a slight accentuation of the hips, stood in the corridor outside. As we passed her, I found myself looking momentarily into a face, fair-skinned, crowned by hair of the tint called golden, a pair of blue and long-lashed eyes—a very attractive ensemble, even though in the brief space wherein our glances crossed I noted what seemed a slight tenseness about her mouth.

Then we were approaching the door of Dorien's suite, and she had vanished into the cage. But I felt I knew her, although I had never knowingly seen her before in my life.

"Do you know who that was?" I glanced at Jim.

He nodded. "Sure. She was visitin' Dorien, an' she made it a point to lamp us as she was gettin' out. He's apt to be in a cordial humor if we've run his sweetie off. Johnson was right—she ain't a bad looker, an' she certainly knows how to dress."

I nodded also. The girl's appearance had actually surprised me, lacking much as it did of those subtle earmarks, one comes through experience to consider the stigmata of vice. But I made no verbal comment as I set my finger to the little mother of pearl button let into the frame of the door of Dorien's suite.

The door itself was opened promptly by a short and rather heavy-set Jap.

"Misser Dorien, yessir," he said with no particular inflection, but inspecting us with darkly glinting eyes. "Hats—please."

"All right, Togo," Jim said as he passed his over.

"Kato, sair—excoose," the man corrected with a flash of teeth. "Theese way." He led out of a small reception hall into a living room beyond it, where Dorien sat.

At least one supposed the man in a huge chair placed with its back to a window was Dorien himself, for he resembled in both physique and feature, Dual's assumed description of the night before. And the room itself carried out that hint of Dorien's love of beauty, his luxurious instincts Semi had suggested. It was a surprisingly happy combination of man's living quarters, and in some cases bizarre yet decidedly charming *objets d'art*.

I smiled, too, as Kato gave us seats, facing his employer. One could hardly escape the fact that their position left Dorien's face half-shadowed, ours exposed to the full play of the light. Quite evidently, then, in so much the interview was staged.

Not until we were seated did Dorien give the least sign of a recognition, and then he spoke in an almost petulant fashion: "Excuse my not rising. I presume you know I was injured some time ago, and am still rather weak. State your business as briefly as possible, if you don't mind, and—mention your names, of course."

I complied, introducing Jim and myself, and assenting to his assumption that we knew of his recent illness.

He frowned. "Private investigators?" he repeated. "And—just how am I to understand the word. Do you think my private affairs need investigating or intend to suggest that I employ you to run down the affairs of others? What brings you here, Glace?"

"Why," said Bryce before I had framed an answer, "it's like this. We know you was shot on th' mornin' of May fifteenth an' pretty nearly croaked. An' we know you're rich. An' we know there was a woman. An' we know you haven't squealed. Looks like blackmail, Dorien—"

The man in the chair set his lips. One could see him stiffen slightly, gather himself together as it seemed.

"You know quite a lot," he interrupted, "each and every detail of which knowledge you could have gained from the police. They've already interviewed me, and I told them to mind their own business till they were asked to help. I'm the man who was shot, I take it, and I don't feel the need of any private 'dicks.' You've got a devilish nerve to try to force your way into the matter—"

"But hold on, Mr. Dorien," Jim broke into what seemed to me more a deliberately built up bluster than a sincerely voiced emotion, "we thought you might like to run the matter out. Of course you wouldn't want to call in the Central Office in a private matter—especially when there was a girl, but—"

"Run what out?" Dorien snapped, sitting up in his chair.

"Why—run down this mob—fight back," Jim suggested.

"What mob?" our involuntary host challenged directly.

"Why—Kelley's mob, of course—"Jim met both the question and Dorien's eyes.

"And—who is—Kelley?" Dorien took time, and when he spoke his voice was once more cold.

"Why—the man who set th' girl on you." Jim smiled slightly—just a mere momentary twitching of the lips, as one might smile who held a fairly comprehensive knowledge another pretended not to possess. "He got a busted arm about the same time you was hurt."

That was pulling it pretty fine, because Bryce didn't actually know just when or where Kelley's arm had been broken, but even in the shadow I saw Dorien's cheeks flush slightly and then go white. He breathed deeply.

"Don't you think it quite probable that several other persons in a city of this size may have met injuries on the same or an approximate date?" he responded, drawling. And suddenly he laughed. "You've built up a lovely house of cards, haven't you, Bryce. Is it a sample of how you work? If it is, leave your card with Kato as you go out. I may need you some time, when I want to hunt mares' nests—or some equally hypothetical object. But—I've enjoyed your visit. In a way—what with its intimation of blackmail and gangsters and all that—it's been quite Nick Carteresque."

And now it was Bryce who flushed. He puffed out his stubby brown mustache. Myself I felt a half inclination to echo Dorien's laughter—the mocking change that had come into being in his expression. Dual had said he could be sarcastic, and apparently he could. Plainly he had the best of the matter thus far, and knew it, and the knowledge left him amused. Bryce appeared to know it, too, to judge by the tinge in his cheeks, but he kept cool and played his hand after a momentary pause:

"Lookin' at it your way, I reckon it does look a bit like melo or even rotten drama, but—I've seen a lot of pretty rotten stuff in my life, an' lookin' at it my way, the line of chatter you're pullin' sounds mighty much like bluff. If I was a bull, I reckon you'd act different—"

"If?" Dorien interjected, his lips relaxing into a half grin though his lids were narrowed. "Why the subjunctive? Perhaps you are." One could fancy him recalling the words of the youth we had met below stairs to that effect.

But Jim actually stared. "Huh! What gave you that sort of a notion?" he countered gruffly.

"Frankly, your intelligence, I'm afraid." Dorien laughed again.

And surprisingly Bryce chuckled. "I'll admit our intelligence don't seem to jibe worth a cent, but—that's another card house, an'—with equal frankness, Mr. Dorien, you're down on a dead card."

"Then who are you? Who sent you here?" Dorien demanded, leaning forward.

"Well—somebody who knew a lot more about th' inside of this works than I'd have been willin' to guess at," Bryce said with a lack of hesitation that matched the grin upon his face.

Right there I saw an opening and took it. While Jim and the man in the chair had been matching wits, I had not been mentally idle myself. And even while I kept track of their verbal sparring, I had been running over our conversation with Semi the night before. Now, as Bryce suggested him, his words chosen, as I felt, to excite an entirely different understanding in Dorien's mind, things appeared all at once to match up. Furthermore, there was a slight even if transitory indication that Jim had at least given the man before us food for thought.

He sat for an instant boring Bryce with an intent gaze before he leaned back again in his chair with a somewhat sneering twist of his lips.

"Doesn't it occur to you," I said, "that one might assume your disinclination to speak with any freedom of this matter, to be induced by a possible desire of protecting the woman in the case?"

For a moment he did not answer, and then he asked a question: "Are you too possessed by this conception of a gang—a blackmailing mob?"

"It appears plausible, does it not?" I retorted.

"And—you assume—I note that you allege it is an assumption—that I am refraining from any action save that of minding my own business in the matter, because of a desire to shield the girl they set to lead me on to a place where they could extort hush money from me? Rather far-fetched, Mr. Glace."

"Unless we make another assumption."

"And that?"

"That she succeeded in arousing your interest very deeply."

He frowned again, and I saw the fingers of a hand contract on the arm of his chair.

I went on before he even attempted to answer. "Let us further assume that in seeking to infatuate you she found herself caught in a reciprocal regard."

"Oh, good Lord! Pray spare me your assumptions. You're worse than your partner," he burst out with a force that made his first words actually rasping. "See here—I've had enough of this. Kato will show you out."

"In just a moment," I protested, wondering if after all we were going to fail wholly. I played what I felt was my final card. "Let us assume further that as a result of everything that has happened, she finds herself now in opposition to the very people she has been serving. They would hardly take such an attitude on her part kindly. Considering all my assumptions, you would hardly be apt to follow any save your present course."

"Oh, slush!" Bryce surprised me with a disgust-inflected objection. "Dorien ain't th' sort to lay off simply in order to save th' hide of that sort of a woman—a girl that's been used to shake down a bunch of suckers by a mob. He's got personal reasons, of course—"

"You're damned right!" Dorien exploded. "Furthermore, Miss Roamer is not at all what you think."

"Who?" Bryce's tones were suddenly purring.

"Why, Miss Roam—Miss Roma Temple. It's no secret that she was here at the time I was shot, I believe."

Dorien shrugged, but for just an instant he lost poise. Jim had touched him on a sensitive point and he had winced, and in wincing he had slipped, even though he had recovered with a remarkable facile quickness and retrieved or attempted to retrieve his error cleverly enough. I saw his chest rise over a deep drawn inhalation as he paused, saw added caution and an unspoken question looking at me out of his eyes.

I nodded. "Oh, yes, we know she was here at that time, Mr. Dorien, of course."

Abruptly he shook his head. "Glace—you're as bad as a diplomat, really. One might imagine that you were an embassy sent by this mob of—Kelley's, I think Bryce said the name was—to warn me that the girl was apt to take harm if I made a move."

"Oh, dear me," said Bryce. "Who's melodramatic now? But— we saw her in the hall as we came in here, and I don't mind sayin' she ought to be valuable to Kelley. She made a hit with me myself."

Dorien came halfway out of his chair.

"Damn it all!" His voice rose almost to a treble. "Will you two get to hell out of here or do I have to call Kato and let him use a little jujutsu on you both?"

"Oh, we'll go—we'll go," Jim responded, rising. "Don't go off half-cocked. When a man does he's apt to spill something he's meant to keep to himself. And here's somethin' to chew on. We ain't connected with th' police, an' Kelley didn't send us, neither. You can tell Miss *Roamer* that, too, when you ring her up at th' Kenton. She'll probably ask you what it was all about."

He turned toward the door into the hall. "This way out?"

"Yes. Use it," Dorien flung back from between tight set teeth. His hands were clenched, his voice choked.

"Shall I call Kato?" Bryce suggested.

"No—get out!"

"What was the use of rubbing it in, and why tell him we

didn't come from Kelley, after half persuading him we had?" I inquired after we had regained the street.

Bryce grinned. "It don't do any harm to keep th' other feller guessin', m'son. That's one thing I learned when I was on th' force. I reckon you got it?"

"Oh, yes," I said, "I got it. The Temple girl is also known as Roamer."

"Yep. An' th' minute I started to pan her, Dorien slipped. He's more'n a little interested in that blond skirt. Well—Semi said straws showed which way the wind blew or broke a camel's back. That guy's guv us a straw, I reckon, an' now all we got to do is to find a camel." Jim chuckled deep in his throat.

CHAPTER V

A NEW ELEMENT

THAT WAS EASY enough to say, but personally I couldn't see that we were any closer to the actual event than we had been as we caught a car back down town. Of course learning that the name the girl was using for the nonce was no more than an alias—that the name Dorien had mentioned might be anything from a second pseudonym to hers by birth, was something. Still I couldn't see that it greatly helped, except in its indication that Dorien was caught in the mesh of her physical charms which I was ready to admit were great.

"That's a good deal like the classic recipe for cooking a rabbit, isn't it?" I remarked. "First catch your—camel."

"Oh, sure," my companion assented.

"But—I ain't certain Dorien didn't give us a couple other straws. Dual said he was likely to be a pretty good liar, and he is. But—he ain't quite good enough. There's a mob. There was that stuff he pulled on you about bein' sent to warn him. He was feelin' for somethin' when he shot that at you. You could see it in his eyes. He knows Kelley, an' I wouldn't wonder if he knew his arm was broke. He was stallin' from first to last or I'm a harness bull an' never was anything else, even if they did use to write inspector before my moniker on th' city pay roll."

"Well, yes," I said. "There's that. But he knows now we weren't sent to warn him."

"Oh, no, he don't," said Bryce. "He knows we were sent by

somebody with quite a bit of info—or he thinks he does—an'
he'll be tryin' to dope us out. Besides, it's likely to help Dan."

"Just how?" I asked. Whatever he was, Jim was no fool, no
matter how he might wander in his talk.

"Why"—his dark eyes twinkled—"Dorien an' th' girl will
have a talk. She knows we went there. She'll have to know why.
She's a woman, ain't she? An' when neither of them knows
nothin' about it really, she'll be considerably jazzed. I don't know
what Dan's play is any more than you do, but—th' more restless
she is th' easier it ought to be for th' kid to reach her."

I nodded.

Not the least surprising thing about that was to find Bryce
dabbling with no little insight into the psychology of the situation as affecting Roma Temple.

"Well, perhaps it might have that effect upon her," I said.

"There ain't no perhaps about it," he retorted. "There's a lot
about this business we don't know an' just for a guess she ain't
too easy in her mind, after such a run in as they must have had.
Didn't Semi say she was at war with herself?"

"Yes," I admitted, "he did."

"Well, then—he's probably coached Dan in just about how
she's to be approached."

I sighed. "Probably, yes." It would certainly have been unlike
Dual to have sent the boy on such a mission without having
carefully outlined his course of procedure in advance.

We left the car and caught a cage up to our office.

Johnson sat in my private den, and there was that about him,
an air of suppressed excitement, sufficient to indicate that he
had something on his mind.

"Hello," he greeted our appearance. "Been coolin' my heels
here for an hour. Where have you two been?"

Jim told him and he grinned. "Dual sent you over there?" he
said. "Well, did you succeed in making him loosen up?"

Between us we put him in touch with what had occurred,

and at the end he nodded. "Roamer, eh? Well, there ain't such a lot to that, I guess. Nothin' strange in her havin' one or a dozen monikers, is there?"

"No-o," Bryce conceded, "there ain't. Th' peculiar thing is Dorien's callin' her by that one, when she's been registered at th' Kenton as Temple all along. Where'd he get it unless she gave it to him, and why did she do that? If it's nothin' but an alias, what's her game? Then, too, he's as sensitive about her as a sore tooth."

Johnson eyed him. "Maybe you might be, too, if you'd sat in his sort of game. As to what she's up to, I don't know any more than you do, of course, but here's another thing an' th' real reason for my comin' up. I stumbled onto somethin' last night an' this afternoon, that gave me a pretty good notion they was done with Dorien. What do you think that dame did last evenin'?"

He paused as though to assure himself of our attention rather than for any answer and immediately went on: "Naturally, I've got a man with an eye out in her direction besides your boy Dan. He's a clever kid, an' he may succeed in bringin' Dual in touch with that jane. But I got a shadow on her just th' same. So along around six she comes out of th' hotel dressed to about a minute ahead of th' style, hops into a taxi and beats it down to a café an' meets a man, an' they have dinner in a private room."

"This Temple girl does?" said Jim while I felt my interest quicken.

"Yep."

"An' did your man know th' feller she met by any chance?"

"Yes. His name's Kornung."

"Who?"

"Hubert Kornung—one of th' biggest, if not th' biggest, man in his line in town. He's a consulting engineer, moves in th' best circles, an' from what I hear is quite a ladies' man, though he's never married. Old enough to be th' girl's father an' reported wealthy." Johnson broke off with a disgusted sort of grin.

"But—my aunt!" Bryce exploded. "You don't mean this gang

have got crust enough to start anything more of that sort at this time?"

"Crust?" Johnson repeated gruffly. "They've got crust enough, I reckon. But that ain't exactly th' point. Dorien ain't talkin' an' it's nearly a month since he was shot. Besides, I don't guess they know we're watchin'. I haven't exactly been on th' job with a band. Of course I went to see Dorien, but he told me to stay off, an' since then there hasn't been any move they know of. So I don't know as it's exactly a question of crust. Th' way it looks to me, they simply fell down in th' Dorien matter, an' are startin' a new deal."

"Meanin' they failed to connect with any coin?" Bryce suggested.

"Sure. I don't reckon they got anything out of him considering what happened. That may have been what started the rough house, too—"

"That or the girl," said Jim.

"Oh, lay off on th' girl for a minute," Johnson grunted. "Here's another little thing. Last night she takes dinner with Kornung, an' I bumps into Kelley hangin' around th' neighborhood of th' Kenton this afternoon. I tips my man to watch him an' along right after three his report comes in. Sure enough th' girl blows up from somewhere just about three, an' Kelley tacks onto her an' they go into th' hotel. An' now get this into your bean. This mornin' I dug it out of the night elevator boy at Monks Hall that he took this skirt up to Dorien's room around twelve th' night before th' shootin'.

"Maybe you see what that means. She was planted. Her play was to be there when th' guy who was to make th' big noise an' grab th' bank roll showed up. An' why should Dorien have been shot over her, when she was only doin' what had been planned all along. More probably he acts up rusty. He an' that Jap of his may even have tried to throw th' feller out—"

"Like he offered to do with Gordon an' me this afternoon!" Bryce interrupted quickly.

"Sure," once more Johnson nodded. "An' in th' mix-up he gets shot, an' Kelley gets a broken arm."

"By granny!" Jim exclaimed. "An' that's all he does get, I reckon."

"Naturally," Johnson assented, "what with Dorien shot in th' head among other little details."

"An'"—Jim narrowed his lids and pursed out his mustache—"that brings us back to this other thing th' way you see it. Havin' failed to make a clean-up there, they may feel th' need of makin' another turn, So they look around an' pick on Kornung—"

"Just about." Once more Inspector Johnson grinned.

It was plausible enough, too, all things considered, if one knew anything about the so-called badger game. Every once in a while that sort of an enterprise has a habit of going wrong. Wherefore as Johnson plainly believed, the gangsters who had met a defeat in the Dorien instance could only put into practice the oft-repeated admonition to "try, try again." And right there in my considerations was where the usage of long custom stepped in.

"Don't you think," I remarked, "that in view of the fact that Dual is really directing this matter, we're rather wasting time in sitting here trying to thresh things out ourselves?"

"By granny, yes." Jim got out of his chair with an alacrity flattering to my suggestion to say the least. For a few moments following Johnson's exposition of the latest developments with which he had come into contact, he had been simply sitting and chewing on the butt of an unlighted cigar.

"Then come along." I rose.

Johnson followed me up.

Five minutes later we mounted the bronze-and-marble staircase from the twentieth floor to the roof.

Dual sat there, beside the little fountain, the strongly framed form of a man clad in his white and purple robes. At the sound of the chimes he glanced up and stood to greet us.

"Welcome, my friends. And you, Mr. Bryce—did you and

Gordon possibly garner a bit of grain from a somewhat barren field?"

Jim's lips quirked slightly. "Well—I think we got a straw or two," he returned, "but I don't know how it's goin' to run in wheat. Johnson here has a line out, too, on what looks right now like a field of pretty wild-oats."

Dual smiled. "Sit down and tell me," he invited. "I was but sitting here in contemplation of the beauties of creation. And now I shall listen to the fresh vagaries of the Creator's noblest work and his most rebellious, since it is man alone who so abuses the intelligence with which he is endowed that he fails to draw a lesson from the flowers with which I have decked my garden or the bees that flit above them, in tune with an Infinite God."

We told him, each in his own way, each adding a little to the total. And he heard us as was his custom without any interruption. Beside us the fountain tinkled and the goldfish flashed, the lilies opened their golden hearts to the gold of the westering sun. Beyond us the tower stood in white and classic outline. It came to me that we sat there like neophytes in the presence of some master of a philosophy grown ancient—so ancient indeed that it had been largely forgotten or cast aside by a busy world—and yet a thing that lived, although forgotten, thrust aside. Dual, in his robes of white and purple, was still the learned teacher, by whose lips its living truths were voiced.

Briefly the spell of the concept held me, and then it was Semi himself who broke it:

"There are times when the understanding of man grows confused in the contemplation of some matter by reason of a seeming conflict of purpose, wherein man's understanding differs from that of his Creator. For whereas man seeks to harmonize reason with mere appearance—the purpose back of all manifestation establishes reason within the works of the All Mind. You may recall that yesterday I offered the opinion that the matter with which we are concerned would prove both contradictory and involved. And in so much we find the woman known both as Temple and Roamer by the man against whom it appears her efforts were exerted. And we find him both sensitive toward a derogatory mention of her, and still in association with her. And again we find her apparently bound to the gangster Kelley, whom Mr. Johnson regards as the head of a blackmailing organization in which she has already served.

"In addition she dines last night with a man by the name of Kornung, and Mr. Johnson therefore suggests that the band have set some fresh scheme on foot, offering in support of his contention his belief that the Dorien episode was without monetary results. In the latter assumption I am ready to concur, since my study of Dorien's astrological charts has led me to the conclusion that he actually suffered no major financial loss."

"And there you are!" Johnson declared with a glance at Bryce and myself that showed his inward elation. "Dorien simply wouldn't kick in on the showdown, an' they mixed it. But he don't squeal, an' as soon as they get their breath they start another piece of work."

"Quite a natural conclusion," said Semi Dual. "Let us then consider Kornung. You have named him a consulting engineer, Mr. Johnson. In what particular branch of engineering may I ask?"

"Why, civil," Johnson told him. "Mainly construction work, I believe. Before he got so high up, I understand he did quite a lot of work in the West."

"And do you know anything of further interest about him?"

"Nothin' except that he's been here for ten or twelve years, but—I guess that ought to be enough for the present."

Johnson's expression was actually smug, and I could hardly blame him. His discovery seemed to have riveted Dual's attention.

"For the present at least, save perhaps his personal appearance. You are acquainted with it?" Dual inclined his head.

"Oh, yes. I know how he looks all right. He's dark, with a wide an' thin-lipped mouth an' iron-gray hair th' past few years.

Got a prominent forehead an' walks with a stoop that makes him look like his head was too heavy. 'Bout five feet nine, I should say at a guess, an' wide shouldered."

"All of which, taken with his occupation," said Semi Dual, "would seem to indicate a child of Saturn."

"Huh?" Johnson grinned. "Well—probably if you say so, though I ain't pretendin' to understand you, when you go to draggin' in th' name of stars."

"Nor do I expect you to do so," Dual returned, "since each man reads but what he may according to his light. Yet in the inverted bowl we call the sky, the stars are points of light by whose aid man may arrive at a fuller understanding of many things, provided he reads aright."

"Oh, I ain't denyin' that," Johnson began.

And Semi checked him. "As I know, Mr. Johnson. Wherefore I shall venture an opinion that even though Kornung walks with his eyes upon the ground, yet he should carefully watch his steps, and further, that in view of what you yourself have told me, and the matter on which we are mutually engaged, Mr. Hubert Kornung should be considered a very good man— to watch."

He spoke slowly, carefully as was his way, weighing, as it seemed, each word, seeking as one might think to give each its proper value, to neither run beyond nor fall short of an exact measure—to offer as it were a tentative appraisal of this newer element in the problem presented for his solution than anything else—not to assert or affirm more than was warranted by a present knowledge. And I, who knew him, read into his every intonation, his bearing, a deeper, hidden, even cryptic something to be taken out and read perhaps even as he himself had inti- mated, by the light of the wheeling stars.

Johnson, however, seemed wholly satisfied. "An' I guess I can understand th' last part of that without any trouble. I'll watch him," he said with unmistakable force, and laughed a trifle grimly as he rose.

CHAPTER VI

DAN ON THE WIRE

"**DID YOU GET** it?" Johnson went on, when we had gone down and were waiting for a cage.

"Oh, yes," said Bryce, "we got it, didn't we, Glace?"

I nodded. "He wants Kornung shadowed from now on until something turns up." In so much Semi's intention was past any question.

Johnson chuckled. He was in high good humor. "You bet. And he's goin' to get what he wants. I'll say he is. He certainly is th' limit. Kornung wants to watch his step. That's puttin' it into a mighty few words."

"An'," Jim added, "in watchin' th' man they're tryin' to get, we may get th' gang that's tryin' to get him. Sort of th' biter bit, or th' getter got. Well, things are beginnin' to move."

"Yes," Johnson nodded. "An' before night I'll have a man on th' job to help get th' getter. Boys, we're goin' to bust that gang wide open. Unless somethin' slips, we're goin' to get 'em."

"An' speakin' of slippin'," Bryce suggested, "if that girl should take a notion to tell Kelley about our callin' on Dorien this afternoon, I reckon it might."

"Damnation!" Johnson's air of complacency collapsed. "Well—if you two have mussed this up—"

"If we have?" Jim retorted. "Dual sent us over there, and he said this thing was full of contradictions, an' I guess he's right. Go put your man on Kornung, an' keep your shirt on. You dragged us into this yourself."

"Yes, I know I did," Johnson assented gruffly in a way that half intimated that he wished he had not. "Well, come along. Here's a cage."

As a matter of fact, there had been several while we stood there, but we followed him into it as he led the way, and left him on the seventh floor, with a perfunctory word of parting to which, as much as anything else, I attributed my partner's grin once we were inside my room again.

"Johnson's a good bull," he said as he threw himself into a chair and lighted a cigar. "But just because Dual tells him to watch Kornung's no reason why he should swell up like a poisoned pup. An' even admittin' that he turned up what looks like a good lead, he's got no cause to get peeved. That girl may tell Kelley about seein' us this afternoon, an'—she may not. What was it Semi said about wheels?"

" 'Wheels within wheels, and who can say where their course shall run?'" I repeated.

And he nodded. "Well—th' answer ain't Johnson for a bet, nor yet me; but—wheels within wheels is a pretty good way to describe this thing, I guess, what with th' girl usin' two names at once, an' trottin' around with Kelley, an' takin' dinner with Kornung, an' goin' to visit Dorien, an'—see here, you ain't forgettin' that stuff about Venus Dual pulled last evening, are you?"

"No, Jim, I'm not," I said. Because frankly I had been recalling Semi's statement from time to time ever since he had made it, as applying to the girl we had seen just before we entered Dorien's suite some hours before. "And furthermore, do you notice that Roma is sufficiently like Roamer to suggest the possibility that one was built from the other?"

"Holy—smoke!" Jim literally blew up. His eyes widened and his jaw appeared to sag. "Son, that's right, an' she told Dorien her name was Roamer at a guess. At that it may be her right one. Because, see here—we've been forgettin' something else Semi said. Didn't he say she was in opposition to Neptune in

Dorien's figure? An' ain't it reasonable to suppose that what he meant by that is that th' girl's in two minds at once?"

"Quite possibly," I assented, "since he also asked me if a person might not be held to be in trouble when they were at war with themselves?"

"Yep," Jim nodded. "An' he didn't deny it either when I asked him if he meant she an' Dorien were in love. Oh, Pip! Wheels within wheels is right. I'm gettin' 'em in my head. Didn't Dual say, too, that Dorien might see th' best there was in th' woman an' take her into his house? An' didn't Johnson say she was there when he was shot, like th' literal cuss he is? Say, how's this? Change house to heart—an' you've got th' real meanin'—what Semi really meant. It's th' best part of her is in love with that guy an' th' worst part that's been used by this here Kelley an' his mob."

For a moment I did not answer, because what he had said actually ran very close to some of my own thoughts. Sitting there, I tried to recall Semi Dual's exact words, to harmonize them even if in slight degree with what I knew of his art. Each division of the zodiacal circle, as I recalled, was known as a house. And if one actually changed the word to heart, as Bryce suggested, what other interpretation would there be to Semi's assertion save that of love? Love, then, between the man and

the woman, who had been so differently thrown together, and—
the very soul of the woman, divided against itself. It wasn't
exactly a pleasant picture. A thing of that sort never is. And
yet—it hinted of a possible cause behind a great deal that we
already knew had happened—it even offered an explanation of
Dual's assertion that largely by the influence of this woman had
Dorien's life been saved. In the end I voiced the literal truth:

"I don't know, Jim. Possibly you're right."

"As a matter of fact," he said, "I ain't no Joseph when it comes
to interpretin' such things, but I got a hunch that guess is pretty
warm, as we used to say when we was kids. Didn't Dorien say
she wasn't th' sort we thought her? An' wouldn't that look like
he was sweet enough on her to mean it, or that she had him
fooled, or both?"

"Oh, I'll admit all that," I told him, "but what about this
Kornung business then?"

"Kornung?" Jim repeated and lapsed silent, appearing to study
the tip of his cigar. When he finally went on he prefaced his
words with what hardly seemed profanity and was yet an oath.
"Damn it! Johnson said this was a filthy business, an' it is.
They've got her"—he opened and closed his fingers slowly,
doubling them into his palm with an apparent gripping force—
"like that. She's worked their little games for them before—an'
they got her, Glace."

Once more his words impressed me.

"You mean Kelley pulls the strings?" I said.

And once more he nodded. "Sure—it's sort of like that
Rubber-at of that Old Mark—K.M."

"What?" I stammered.

"Well, you say it. That Persian poet Semi's always quotin'."
He gave me a sheepish grin.

"Do you mean Omar Khayyám?" I suggested.

"Yes. That stuff about shows an' shadows an' lanterns—sort
of a marionette performance th' way I always took it. How does
it go?"

"We are no other than a moving row
Of Magic Shadow Shapes that come and go
Round with the Sun Illumined Lantern held
In Midnight by the Master of the Show."

I quoted the quatrain, and he nodded again at the end:

"That's it, an' th' way I see it Kelley's th' master of this particular pantomime. Didn't he meet her this afternoon an' probably go to her rooms with her for a chin, or to see how she an' Kornung were comin' on? Great cat!"

He broke off and sat puffing out his mustache above the cigar clamped into the corner of his mouth.

"What's the matter now?" I questioned.

"Dan!" he resumed, still in exclamatory fashion. "Say—ain't it th' devil how when Semi sits into a deal he always draws a full house?"

I smiled. Jim's words were, to say the least, graphic, and, being in their way somewhat symbolic, quite naturally suggested something else. More than once before this I had noted the uncanny way in which some move of our strange friend's led by a positiveness of result that could scarcely be classed as coincidence merely to some development militating strongly to his success. Dan had been planted at the Kenton for the avowed purpose of bringing him in touch with Roma Temple, and yet here inside of twenty-four hours, Kelley, the suspected gangster, walked into the hotel with her and—there was that arrangement of the telephone in her room of which Dan had told us himself. If the adjustment had been made—if Kelley went to the girl's quarters with her—I looked straight back into my partner's eyes.

"That kid," I said. "If he sees them and slips into the adjoining room—"

He interrupted me, grinning. "Oh, splash me, yes. You an' Johnson an' me is all a bunch of shadows, I reckon. Dual's th' real master of this show. It was his notion to rig that telephone up to work like a dictograph. An' look what happens. Right off th' bat Kelley walks in with th' girl to have a talk. Son—something's gettin' ready to break."

"At least," I said, striving to curb a sense of anticipation evoked by his words, "it is likely that Danny will report."

And as though my declaration had cued it, the buzzer of the standard telephone on my desk whirred sharply.

I answered its summons: "Glace speaking."

And then I was listening to Dan: "Hello, Mr. Glace, this is Quinn—an' I got an ear full; but I can't get away from here till eight. Fix it up with Mr. Dual for me to see him about that time, will yuh? That girl sent me out on an errand, but—I left her a book to read, an' I gotta get back."

"Very well, Dan," I promised, "I'll fix it. You've got something, have you?"

"I've got that much at least," he avowed with a youthful importance. "But—I guess it's goin' to be up to th' man on th' roof to unscramble th' egg. Say—you an' Mr. Jim be up there, too, why don't you? I'll stop at th' office. S'-long. That kid's got a peach of a headache, she says, an' I'm afraid that book will make it worse. I went blind on th' first page I read."

His receiver banged up. I hung up my own and repeated the conversation to Bryce.

He frowned. "Book—what book?"

"I don't know," I confessed. "But from what Dan says, it would appear to be something he can't understand, and he left it with Miss Temple while he ran out to a drug store to get her some headache powders, at a venture, and also to use a phone."

"She's got a headache," said Bryce. "Kelley was there, an' she's got a headache now he's gone. Dan heard somethin', Gordon—he heard somethin', I tell you. That boy ain't sleepin' on th' job. Well—hadn't you better call up Dual?"

I turned to the box of the private telephone on the wall. I buzzed and stood waiting until Semi's voice came back in an interrogative "Yes?" along the wire.

And then I told him that Dan wanted to see him shortly after eight.

"I shall expect him," he replied; "and you, my friends, also, if you desire."

"We'll be there." I accepted the invitation, and swung around to Bryce. "Come along, Jim, let's get our dinner. We've got a date for this evening."

He got up and reached for his hat. We went down to the street, and there I left him, after arranging to meet him at the office between seven thirty and eight, and wait for Dan.

I caught a car and rode out home. And once there, I told Connie, my wife, about how the day had gone. She knew Dual personally; had even worked with him in the past, and I frequently talked over with her cases in which both he and we had a hand.

"That girl's in trouble," she declared, after I had explained the situation. "Anybody can see that with half an eye. But Mr. Dual will help her if he feels that she deserves it. He's everybody's friend."

"That's a pretty large contract," I said. "Everybody's friend is nobody's friend, I believe."

She grinned. "And you know very well that's not at all what I mean. He's everybody's friend, just as the sun and the rain fall on rich and poor and good and bad, and he makes a lot that we call right seem wrong, and much that we think is wrong seem right, and—"

"You're getting almost as cryptic as he is at times, don't you think?" I interrupted.

"No," she denied emphatically, "I'm not. He combines goodness and kindness, and sympathy, and understanding, and liberality and—and—decency, with common sense. And he's the only man I ever met who does. And—and—if that girl is really in love with Dorien, and doesn't want to go on with these rotten schemes and that—Kelley tries to make her, why Dual will help her. Didn't he tell Dan he would?"

"I suppose," I retorted as she paused for breath, "that you think he'll knock th' 'l' out of Kelley?"

"You're real funny, and' awfully stale, aren't you?" she sniffed. "Kelley wants to look out, while Kornung watches his step. But I don't think anybody can knock 'th' l' out of anybody unless he wants it knocked out himself."

"Neither does anybody else who knows very much about it," I agreed as I pushed back my plate.

I went back, then, and found Bryce waiting with his inevitable black cigar between his lips.

I lighted a cigarette and found a chair. We sat there and smoked, saying very little as those who know one another frequently will, because, as a matter of fact, what Dan might have gained toward the final outcome of the matter was mainly occupying our thoughts.

He came in just after eight, with an eager light in his eyes and on his freckled face.

"Hello," he began quickly. "Well—did you fix it?"

"Why, yes," I returned, "you're expected."

"Goin' up?" he shot a further query at me.

"We're invited, so I think we'll accompany you, Dan," I told him.

He swung on his heel as I finished. "All right. Come along, then," he said.

CHAPTER VII

DANNY REPORTS

JUST FOR THE moment Dan was pretty much business, decidedly primed with the importance of his appointment and what he brought to it. But as we followed him out and closed the door and stood beside the elevator shaft, he became more just an excited kid.

"Gee," he breathed, "but things have been breakin' my way this afternoon for fair—an' them other bellhops down there—I got 'em puzzled. They know somethin's in th' air but they don't know what it is."

"Steady, young sleuth," said Jim. "Don't get 'em to guessin' too hard. What folks don't know won't hurt 'em, unless they get to wantin' to know too much."

Danny's eyes widened swiftly and then narrowed. "Oh, gee, Mr. Jim," he said again. "I ain't goin' to tip over th' beans. But they can't help wonderin' why it is I always answer that kid's rings; but now that I've got next to her, I won't do that so much—only just enough."

"You have got next to her?" Bryce gave me a glance.

"I'll say I have," said Danny. "She was ripe for most anything this afternoon, an' I took th' chance when I saw it, an' I put it over. Wait till you hear how it worked."

We mounted to the garden, two men and a boy in whose eyes still burned the light of opening vistas of life and its endeavors, straining upward beside us as eager, in this new adventure of his, as some high-strung, mettlesome horse, or a young hound held back from a reeking scent, on a leash.

The chimes rang out beneath our feet.

"Gee!" he murmured for the third time. "Ain't that pretty? Mr. Dual sure has got a swell place."

The door of the tower opened before us as a pale rectangle in the summer dusk. We went toward it between beds of drowsy flowers, nodding June roses, golden poppies, perfume distilling heliotrope. A tinkle of falling water came to my ears from the fountain where the goldfish swam, and the pink and white lilies reclined upon their pads. Then all that was behind us and we were crossing the outer chamber toward that inner one where Dual awaited our coming once more beside his desk.

As we took seats he turned his deep gray eyes on Danny, smiling—he was always very tender with children—and swept his avid face with a glance of understanding, before he spoke to him in prompting.

"And now, Daniel, suppose you tell us first what it was you overheard this afternoon between Miss Roma Temple and the man Archer Kell, after he had accompanied her to her rooms."

"Gee!" Dan's eyes widened swiftly, in what seemed an awed surprise, before he went on in a husky whisper. "How'd you know?"

"Very simply," Semi told him. "You see, Johnson has a man outside the hotel, and he saw Archer Kell meet her and enter the hotel with her, and, of course, knowing that you were there, it was easy to suppose that you had followed your instructions after you telephoned you had something to report, and that Miss Temple had a nervous headache."

A grin swept the face of Danny Quinn. "I didn't say It was a nervous headache," he corrected, "but I guess it was. It wasn't long after that crook Kelley left her that she rang. An' you're right, of course. I listened in. Say—that guy thinks he's some cheese, I guess—an' I'd a liked to punch him on th' nose."

"Yes?" Semi once more prompted. "Why so, Daniel?"

"Why—" Dan took a long breath. "Nobody ought to talk to a lady like he done. He blows in with her right after three, an' I dopes it they're goin' to her room as soon as they takes an elevator. So I sneaks up th' stairs. They's inside by then, an' I ducks into th' other room an' gets hold of the phone an' glues it to my ear. An' first thing he's roughin' it up with her for fair an' she's spittin' back at him. D'ye want me to tell you what I heard or th' way I hooked it up or what?"

"Tell us what you heard as nearly as you can," said Semi Dual.

"All right," Danny resumed. "Th' first thing I got was like this:

"He says, 'Nobody ever double-crossed me an' got away with it yet.'

"An' she says: 'I'm not double-crossin' you, Arch—honest. You simply don't understand.'

" 'Oh, I understand, all right,' he sort of sneers. 'I understand a damned sight better than you think, for all you're clever. As long as I was laid up, you managed to put it over, mainly because for a time I didn't think you'd have th' nerve. But I ain't laid up now, an' there's no use stallin'. Joey th' Poke—'

" 'That moll buzzer!' she comes back.

"An' at that he laughs kind of nasty. Well, he's a pretty good shadder. He seen you go into Monks Hall this afternoon.'

" 'Very well,' she says, 'I won't deny it.' An' all at once she sounded just about as safe as a live wire to me, but Kelley didn't seem to mind.

" 'I told you to lay off that bird, didn't I?' he asks, just like maw used to ask me if I'd been sneakin' sumpin' to eat when I was a kid. An' all she says is: 'Well?'

"An' he don't chew on it a second before he hits back at her, speakin' so low I could hardly hear him: 'I've already told you what would happen if you persisted in being a fool. It's not as hard as you might think in this town to get a man bumped off.'"

"What's that?" Bryce interrupted, sitting forward in his chair. "Bumped off? Did he say that, Dan?"

"Sure." Danny nodded.

"Dorien," said Jim. "He knew she'd been over to Monks Hall. An' what did she say?"

"She didn't say nothin' for a time," Dan declared. "An' then: 'It's always been your plan to hire somebody to do your dirty work, hasn't it, Arch?'

"An' he snaps: 'Yes, an' another habit of mine is to keep what I want for myself. I suppose you think you love him an' he loves you—you who have been man bait for years. Why—'

"She blamed near screams at him. 'Stop!' An' then goes on like she knowed she oughtn't to shout. 'Whatever I've been, I've never sold my right to love if I wish.'

"An' he laughs again an' says: 'You're dead right there. I've took good care you didn't. This afternoon isn't th' first time I've had you watched. I've protected you for years. An' you know that as well as I do. Dorien ain't th' first man would have got hurt, my dear, if you'd ever needed that sort of help or happened to get mushy before. Now be sensible. You've been hard-headed mostly. If we team up, we can put most anything over, an' I'm ready to do th' right thing by you any time you say th' word. Haven't we shaved things close enough on this business as it is?'

"An' with that she says sort of quiet: 'I don't know whether we have or not. There was a coupla fancy dicks over at th' hall this afternoon.'

"That jolted him th' way it sounded. 'To see him?' he asks.

"An' she says, 'Yes.'

" 'What did they want?' he wants to know.

"An' she says sort of like she was laffin': 'How do I know? Perhaps Mr. Dorien will tell me if I call him up. Oh, Arch, you're like all the rest of them. One would think after the way you've used women to fool others, you'd know more of the game; but th' leopard can't change his spots, can he? You're just a man. It takes a woman to put it over, don't it?

" 'Can't you see we've got to keep in touch, if we're to know what's going on? That dick, Johnson, wanted him to help him start something our way, and he doesn't seem to have thrown in his hand even though Jack turned him down. But if I pass him up now—well—he's another man, and he isn't married, and you know it isn't th' first time he's been mixed up with a woman, and he doesn't love you just for yourself, my friend.'

"He chews on that for so long I thought maybe he'd died, an' then he says: 'Well—maybe you're right. Anyway, call him up and see what he says an' let me know. An' see here. You know it's because I'm crazy about you that I'm just a man where you're concerned.'

" 'Yes, I know,' she says; 'but you don't want to let it make you crazy about everything. An' I'll tell you this. There won't anything come of this if you keep quiet till it's settled.'"

Once more Dan's face was creased by an impish grin. "An' whad'y' think? Th' big mutt swallows that jus' like any other man an' flops clean over.

" 'I understand you took dinner with Kornung last evenin',"
he says.

"An' she says: 'Yes.'

"An' then there was somethin' I couldn't hear, 'cause all at once it was nothin' but a mumble, he was speakin' so low or had moved off too far from th' phone, an' then th' door bangs shut, an' it sounded like she was cryin', an' I reckon she was, because, I goes downstairs, an' it wasn't long till she rang, an' when I goes up her eyes was red, an' she said she had a headache an' wouldn't I get her some powders. An' right there was where I saw a chance to butt into th' game. So I drops that book you guv me, an' goes to a drug store an' calls up Mr. Glace an' asks him to fix it for me to see you to-night."

Danny paused and caught his breath.

"Well, my aunt," Bryce broke out in comment, "that sure throws quite a lot of light. Th' girl's in love with Dorien, an' Kelley's crazy about her himself. Th' mutt's jealous, an' is holdin' this threat against Dorien over her as a whip. She's sort of between th' devil an' th' deep sea, ain't she?"

"Indubitably, Mr. Bryce," said Semi Dual. "You dropped the little handbook on astrology I gave you, Daniel, and went to the drug store for the powders? What happened when you returned?"

So that was it. In a flash I saw it. He had given Dan some elementary work on his own peculiar method of gaining knowledge, and—the boy had left it in the room of the nerve-strung girl when he went upon her errand. And I knew Bryce saw the subtlety of it also, because just for a moment his jaw appeared to sag, and he closed it grimly as Danny began to speak.

"Why, when I went back she was sittin' there lookin' it over, an' she gives me a funny sort of look an' says: 'Is this yours?' An' I says it is, an' she asks me what I knew about that sort of thing, an' I says not much, but I've got a friend who knows all about it, an' can tell anybody how anything is goin' to happen or when, if he knows when they was born. An' she says, 'Anything? Do you mean that, boy—really?'

"An' I tells her 'Yes'm,' just like Mr. Dual said I should if I could make a chance. 'Far as I know that is—who you're goin' to love, an' when you're goin' to die, an'—whether you're goin' to get married or die an old maid.' An' she says: 'Do you think I'll die an old maid, Danny?' An' I says: 'Not unless th' men is awful foolish.'

"An'—" abruptly Dan stammered, while his freckled face grew red. "Gee—when I said that I'm darned if she didn't reach right out an' grab hold of me an' kiss me—an' I could feel it right down to my toes. She's awful pretty, honest, an' her breath was sort of sweet—an' I could see her eyes was shinin' sort of queer, an' she up an' says: 'You really know somebody who reads horoscopes, Danny?' You see I'd made it a point to tell her my name th' first time she gave me a tip, so she knew it. An' I says yes, I knew somebody, an' it was him had guv me th' book. She sits there an' studies a minute, an' then she asks how much does it cost. So then I tells her it don't cost nothin', but I reckon nobody could get my friend to do it unless he wanted to, because men who do real work of that kind ain't doin' it for money, like these dollar a shot fellers in th' papers.

"She frowns at that an' bites her lip, an' I says: 'But if you'd like him to read yours, I'll ask him. What's th' matter, Miss Temple?' An' she says real quick like: 'Oh, I can't tell you that, dear.' Gosh, first she kissed me, an' then she called me dear. Can you beat it? But she gets up an' goes over to a writin' table an' writes sumpin down, an' seals it up, an' comes back an' gives it to me, an' says: 'Give this to your friend and ask him if he will say what he sees for a girl in trouble.' An—here."

He produced an envelope from a pocket and handed it to Semi.

Dual took it and slit it open, drew out a single folded sheet of paper.

"September 11, 1896," he read aloud. "My friends, we have here the birth date of Roma Temple. Wait." He swung about to face his desk.

Well, it had worked, I thought, as we sat there. Here was the first step. Here once more the man who sat now engaged in his mystic calculations, his reading of Life's actual forces, had proved right in a psychological estimate. The little book on astrology had proved a bait at which the woman, in her hour of mental travail, had caught, and catching, was yet to find herself drawn into the scope of his influence thrown out and about her, to be drawn nearer and nearer to him until at length he and she should stand face to face.

I glanced at Jim. He sat with a half grin, an expression of utter satisfaction on his features. I turned my eyes to Danny, and found his fastened on the strong, calm profile of the worker at the desk, thrown out in perfect silhouette against the golden light. Light and shadow. In a sense it was like the things with which he worked—he who sat there calculating the forecasting shadows before the events of a life.

And then he lifted his head and turned it and—smiled and began to speak: "Nearly forty years ago there appeared a poem from the pen of Susan Marr Spaulding, entitled 'Fate,' a few lines of which I quote before giving the present demonstration of its truth:

> "Two shall be born the whole wide world apart,
> And all unconsciously shape every act
> And bend each wandering step to this one end—
> That one day out of darkness they shall meet
> And read life's meaning in each other's eyes.

"The seventh degree of Capricorn was on the mid-heaven, and Aries was thirteen degrees twelve minutes on her ascendant, at the time of Miss Temple's birth. Mars was the Lord of the Horoscope, conjoined to Neptune, both in Gemini, which was ruled by Mercury set on the cusp of the house of marriage in Libra, one of the signs of Venus, who stands near the cusp of the seventh in her own house. Scorpio is on the cusp of the eighth, and Saturn in Scorpio, with Uranus. These are the elements of the example I wish to translate, and this is their meaning as I read it: We have before us a woman of psychic fire, functioning largely on an intellectual plane, dominated by love when it comes upon her, yet exposed to perils and dangers through her very womanhood—capitalizing the assets of youth and beauty and feminine charm which she possesses, in cold-blooded deliberation for a merely material gain, compelling men to pay her after she has snared them, yet—through the position of her moon—ruler of the cusp of her house of Love and, in conjunction with Saturn, snared in her own trap in the end.

"So much for the indications. But now to justify my quoting of part of Mrs. Spaulding's lines: If we compare her chart with that of Dorien, we shall find that her sun is on the place of his moon, showing a deep attraction between them should they ever meet. Her moon is sextile to her sun, consequently to his moon. His moon and hers are both in conjunction with Saturn. Their Saturns and moons are sextile to each other. His sun is in her mid-heaven, as is her sun in his. His Jupiter is on the cusp of her house of marriage. Her Mars and Neptune in his, and his Uranus in hers. Their suns are in trine. All of her benefics are elevated in his nativity—his are made strong in hers. Truly a wonderful agreement wherein each supplies the need of the other, calls out the best within her or him."

He paused briefly while a smile of almost wistful seeming formed on his strong yet kindly lips. And then he went on:

"And yet men scoff at Fate, and grope in boastful blindness along a path presumably of their choosing, yet one in very truth predestined from the beginning to their feet."

Again he paused and for a time nobody spoke, until Bryce cleared his throat in a premonitory fashion and uttered a characteristic comment. "That settles it, I guess. Once those two come together they just simply stuck like a wad of gum on a park bench to your pants. My gosh—what are you goin' to tell her?"

"This," said Semi Dual, and drew a sheet of paper to him and wrote:

> Though a field bring forth tares for years and lie otherwise barren, yet in God's own time may it be fallowed, so that the plowshare having scored it, and the sower swept his hand across it, it may yet bear a goodly harvest when watered by honest tears.

Having written, he inclosed the sheet in an envelope and extended it to Dan.

"Give this to her, Daniel, and say when she has read it, that to a sincere seeker after knowledge or a soul desiring advancement, the door of the temple stands open, and tell her I told you to tell her exactly that, since a wise man keeps his own counsel nor betrays a knowledge obtained in confidence."

"Gee," said Dan in a hushed sort of way, as he took the note from Semi's fingers and put it away in his coat. And then with a sudden change, a bursting of all restraint, as it seemed, by a swiftly impulsive plea: "You're goin' to help her, ain't you? You have just said she couldn't help lovin' Dorien, or him her, if they ever come together, an' this guy Kelley ain't nothin' but a crook an'—an' he's hazin' her, tryin' to hold her an' make her go on bein' crooked an'—honest, Mr. Dual, I don't believe she wants to. She's—she's nice—an' her eyes weren't bad when she—kissed me. So if you'll just help Mr. Glace and Mr. Jim an' Johnson tie a can on Kelley—"

He broke off panting, and his tense little figure went all at once rather limp.

My eyes turned from him to the man at the desk. The thing was plain. The girl at the Kenton had kissed Danny Quinn— orphan, ex-newsboy, self-sufficient little man-child in the main—and in so doing had won his heart.

And Semi understood. Very gently he smiled at the boy before him and quite as gently he replied:

"Deliver my message to her. She herself must decide. For he who seeks shall find, and he who asks shall receive, if he asks as a little child, because simply of its needs, and from no other motive—no other reason, Danny—just as a hungry little child might cry for a bit of bread. And would a true man give a stone to a hungry child or woman who asked for help? Go now, my boy."

He went, wide-eyed, with a murmured: "Yes, sir. Good night."

"Good night," said Semi Dual. "And you, too, my friends. There is nothing more at present, and I desire to compare yet further this most remarkable parallel between the charts of two human lives."

We left him, strong, calm, somewhat inscrutable as always, and went out and across the garden. The chimes rang mellow behind us, a scale of soft harmony in the night.

Bryce cleared his throat as we reached the bottom of the staircase.

"My Gawd!" he said in a husky tone. "I feel—like I'd been to church."

CHAPTER VIII

THE MAN IN THE CELL

PSYCHOANALYSIS—THE DISSECTION, AS it were, of the soul and mental movements which express themselves in the form of human actions—is a wonderful subject, and one to be approached by none save one of the most delicate and comprehensive understanding as well as sympathetic tact. And I think that in nothing did Semi Dual ever more fully exhibit his mastery of that storehouse of psychic energy, the brain, than in this present case.

Wherefore he sent Danny Quinn back that night to his place at the Kenton in an exalted mood calculated to harmonize with that of the woman, who was exalted also by the wonder of the compelling love come upon her, even while its obstacles left her depressed and nervously on edge.

Surely then Dual could look for a quick, an almost compelling, effect from the note he had given Danny, and his verbal message which hinted at so much more than it expressed. Sinking swimmers clutch at straws, and troubled spirits yearn for sympathy and help. And in Semi's symbolic reply, based on her impulsive appeal through Dan, was at least a possible predication of both.

Such thoughts held me as I made my way home after leaving Bryce. And in the morning I took them up pretty much where I had left off. Danny would go to Roma Temple that morning, and—what would she think, what would she do, after reading Semi's note? Would she see in Dual a source of advice and counsellor in a position wherein she was pulled two ways at once? It was on some such thing that he was counting, in my belief, after the developments of the previous night.

The office door was jerked open just as I reached for the knob, and I found myself facing Jim, quite manifestly coming out.

"Here he is now," he called back to Miss Newell, our chief clerk, the minute he saw me. Then he closed the door and took me by the arm. "Come along, son. I just left word with Nellie to shoot you over as soon as you showed up."

"Where?" I suggested, turning back with him pretty much perforce toward the bank of elevators. His hat was at a rakish angle, and there was the usual cigar in the corner of his mouth.

"Central station. Johnson just phoned," he said shortly. "Wanted us both, but you hadn't come, an'—"

"What's he dug up now?" I asked.

Jim grunted. " 'Nother bird what won't talk, from what he says. Got him last night. Picked him off a fire escape over to Monks Hall."

"Monks Hall?" My mind leaped to Dorien.

"Yep," said Jim, as we stepped into a cage.

"At that rate," I began, once we were making our way toward the station, "Dorien had better lock his windows."

Jim nodded. "Or get that Jap of his a shotgun an' put him on guard. My gosh—what do you know about it? This is some pretty little muss, for a thing that don't make no audible noise. An' here's another guy with a Maxim silencer on his mouth."

I smiled. The disinclination of any of the principals to discuss their actions was certainly an outstanding element in the case.

We reached the station in due time, and asked for Johnson.

The sergeant on the desk, who knew us both, ducked his head toward the door of the detectives' room, opening off the front office. "In there. He's expectin' you," he advised.

Johnson sat at his desk, with a somewhat scowling expression on his features, a somewhat compressed look about his mouth.

"Hello," he said. "Sit down. This bird was on th' escape outside Dorien's window, fumblin' with th' sash, when th' patrolman on th' Hall beat lamps him an' brings him in, of course. They frisked him an' gets nothin' but some small change, a knife an' a gun—automatic—same caliber as that with which Dorien was shot."

"Huh? What's that?" Bryce caught up the final detail quickly.

Johnson nodded. "May mean somethin' or nothin'. Thirty-twos are common enough, but—he tried to shed it, an' our man nipped it. Anyway, he was heeled for trouble from th' way it looks, an' we just booked him on an open charge."

"Wait a minute," I interrupted, and told him the conversation between Roma Temple and Kelley, Dan had overheard.

"Threatened to have Dorien bumped off, did he?" Johnson grumbled when I had finished. "Well, whadje mean—that he was tryin' to make good on that threat? Ain't it rather sudden after tellin' th' girl to lay off? Wouldn't he have waited till she made another move?"

"You'd think so," I admitted. "The point is that you got this man last night. What does he say for himself?"

"He don't say a damned thing of any value," Johnson growled. "That's the devil of this whole business—nobody does. Aside from that, he's pretty darned flip, accordin' to th' desk. When they booked him he gave his name as W. Willie an' his residence as 'out West.'"

"W. Willie?" Bryce repeated.

"Yeh. An' when th' sarge asked him what th' 'W.' stood for, he said 'Weary.'" Johnson's lips quirked. "Oh, he's a wise fish, all right, an' no spring chicken. 'Bout forty-five or six, I guess. But—that out West stuff gave me an idea just th' same, considerin' where he was grabbed, so—I have sent over to the Kenton for that girl; an' when she gets here I'm goin' to let 'em take a slant at each other."

"You've sent for—her?" Bryce stared.

Johnson shrugged. "Oh, just a *request* for her to help us iden-
tify Weary Willie. I admit it's a long chance, but it can't hurt
anything so far as I can see, an'—if they *should* know each
other—" He broke off and rose, "Come along. Let's go."

We accompanied him out of the room and back to the door
of the cell house, where we were passed inside. Still pursuing
his lead, we mounted a staircase of metal treads and came out
on an upper tier, and into the presence of a warder who, at a
word from the inspector, opened a small steel door and led us
down a metal balcony to a cell the door of which he in turn
unlocked in order that we might enter.

We did so, and immediately I experienced something of a
shock. The man who sat on the shelf that answered as a bed
was nearly six feet in height as he rose, and correspondingly
built. But it was not his size so much as his face that arrested
my attention. It was that of a man of some forty-five or six, as
Johnson had said, well featured, under brown hair, with a well
shaped nose, a somewhat large and firmly held mouth, a broad
angled lower jaw, and lined, graved deeply, as it seemed, into
what impressed me as an actual mask of repression maintained
through an unknown span of years. And his eyes were like twin
darkened windows wherein his intelligence had stood on guard
as they swept us. And he said no word.

"Sit down, Weary Willie," Johnson began. "Mr. Bryce an' Mr.
Glace here an' me have come up for a little talk. Want to ask
you some questions, an' th' first one is, what was you doin' on
that fire escape at one o'clock this mornin'?"

The man's answer came in a somewhat dry-toned statement:
"I was trying to get inside?"

"What for?" Johnson's second question came more brusquely.

"To see a man."

"Dorien? You was outside his window."

"Was I?" It was as though the man laughed inside his eyes.
"As a matter of fact, sir, I *was* trying to see Dorien; and I climbed
the fire escape because he refused to see me when I applied in

the regular fashion. As a rule I finish an undertaking once I start."

"Yeh?" said the inspector.

"Yes—unless prevented, of course."

Johnson frowned. "Well," he decided, "I guess that's right, because I checked it up in advance. Th' boy over there says you blew in an' asked for Dorien, an' he wouldn't see you. So you generally finish what you start?"

"Yes."

"You're from the West?"

"Yes to that also."

"Why'd you come East?"

"On business."

"With Dorien?"

"It was my business, sir." Willie's voice was quiet, almost too quiet.

"Why don't you say right out it's none of ours?" Johnson snorted.

"I felt sure you would understand the intent."

I saw Johnson's jaw set and suddenly he changed his entire line of question. "Who taught you to stand up when a bull enters your cell?"

I stiffened. I saw Bryce quicken in attention. But the man on the cot merely smiled. "Why—it's common courtesy to rise on the advent of callers, is it not?"

"Like sayin' 'yes, sir,' as I've noticed you've done once or twice?"

"Yes."

Johnson laughed in a sneering way. Willie had palpably omitted the "sir" from his last answer. His glance leaped to my face and Jim, before he went on. "Deep, aren't you?—deep as a well. But they teach that sort of politeness in jails all over th' country. You been arrested before?"

"Oh, yes," said Willie quite calmly.

"Thought so," Johnson grunted in evident satisfaction. "Old hand. All right. Now, see here, Mr. Weary Willie, I'm gettin' a little bit tired myself. Kelley sent you over there, didn't he? Come on, now, loosen up."

"Kelley?" The man's eyes were blank. "Who the hell is Kelley?" It was the first time his language had failed to be exceedingly well chosen, almost of a cultured type.

And it left Johnson temporarily nonplused as I could see from the tinge of red that crept into his cheeks.

The warder appeared at the door in the pause that followed and addressed him. He rose and went outside. The man on the cot followed his departing figure, then let his glance drift back to mine and smiled again faintly.

"All right." Johnson spoke just outside the door and reappeared. "Kelley," he said, as though replying to the as yet unanswered question, "is a dirty crook who uses women in blackmailin' schemes on guys like this Dorien you was tryin' to bust in on last night. He's a dirty yeller dog, an' I'm goin' to get him—you tell him that for me."

"I sincerely hope you do if he's that sort," the man he addressed replied and paused—as there came a sound of lighter footsteps and the girl we had seen at Monks Hall appeared at the cell door in company with the warder. She was a trifle pale, and I noted the quick rise and fall of her breast, a little quiver of her nostrils, but that was all.

"Stand up—let her look at you," Johnson directed.

Willie obeyed.

Man and woman gazed upon one another.

"Ever see him, Miss Temple?" the inspector questioned.

For a moment she made no answer, and then she shook her head. "No, sir—I never saw him in my life."

Myself I watched the man. He stood unmoved by his cot. His face neither hardened nor twitched.

Johnson swung to him. "And I suppose you never saw her either?"

"No—it is a pleasure now, however." Willie inclined his head slightly.

"That's all," said Johnson gruffly. "Much obliged, Miss Temple, but he was caught last night tryin' to break into Dorien's rooms from a fire escape an' we thought—"

"Last night?" There was no mistake about it. Roma Temple swayed upon her feet, and half put out a hand in support toward the steel wall of the cell, before she controlled herself. "But—why should I know him, even if he was doing anything so utterly foolish?"

I caught her eyes and knew she recognized Bryce and myself. They widened, narrowed with a play of iris and lid. "I—assure you I knew nothing whatever about the occurrence. This is the first I have heard."

"All right," Johnson accepted. "Sorry to have troubled you to come over. Thanks just th' same."

"It's—all right, of course." The girl was white now to the lips as she turned and disappeared, and Willie sank back on his cot and smiled again rather wanly as it seemed to me.

"At least," he said, "she wasn't lying. She didn't know me. I trust you're convinced of that. She's some—friend of Dorien's?"

"Here—cut that!" Johnson flared. "Maybe she didn't know you, but I reckon you know her—all right."

"I?" Willie met his frowning regard with naught save apparent surprise in face and voice. "Because I deduce she knows Dorien? Why, sir—that's natural enough. I'm not a fool—"

"No—but you're stallin' just th' same," Johnson interrupted. "I reckon you've been trained in a school where you've learned to pull that sort of stuff. But—don't think you're foolin' me for a minute, with your blind stares an' your pretty talk. You're a deep one, but—every well has a bottom—"

"Why, yes," said Willie, interrupting. "And every road has an ending, and there's a hole in the bottom of the sea. As it happens I've told you the literal truth. I never saw that young woman in my life."

"All right. All right. Come on, boys." Johnson rose.

We followed him out and back to the detectives' room.

He flung himself into his chair so forcibly that it creaked. "The damnedest thing about this whole business is how everybody puts a safety on his jaws," he burst out. "But one thing's certain, whether he ever saw her or not, he knows who she is, an' he's done time somewhere—an' he ain't forgot what he learned wherever it was he did his stretch."

"An'," Bryce suggested. "when you pulled that about Dorien, it pretty near knocked th' girl off her feet."

Johnson grinned. "Sure. I did that on purpose. If Kelley sent this bird to get him, she's hep now, an' one way to bust a gang is to get 'em to fightin' among themselves. This guy is a cool one, an' it's just possible he's th' guy made th' big play in th' beginnin'. Maybe he's th' feller showed up to claim she was his long lost daughter what Dorien had led out of the straight and narrow—"

"Holy smoke!" Jim sat up.

Johnson nodded. "Says he finishes what he starts, you notice. Well, he didn't croak Dorien th' first time, did he, an' he was packin' th' same caliber gun last night—an' Kelley's jealous as poison, accordin' to your boy's report. Maybe he did tell this ex-con to finish his work, like Glace suggested."

"Except," I said, "that if that was the case, he would hardly have asked for Dorien first. Your hallboy says he did."

"Well, yes." Johnson frowned. "Th' whole thing looks like a bag of food for squirrels. Only this guy ain't a nut. He's deep, like I said, an' he'll bear considerable watchin'."

"Not where he is," said Bryce.

"Where he is?" Johnson eyed him. "Well, hardly. He ain't no good where he is, I guess. An' that girl will warn Dorien now that she knows what was tried out last night, especially if she's as stuck on him as your friend Dual thinks. So—I'm goin' to spring him. I'm goin' to give him his hat an' his small change an' turn him out—an'—watch him."

He lifted a heavy hand and sent it crashing down in a clenched fist upon his desk.

CHAPTER IX

IN WILLIE'S LODGINGS

"**I'LL WATCH HIM,**" Johnson went on. "There'll be a man on him th' minute he leaves here, an' he'll see where he goes. He hangs out somewhere, an' naturally he'll head back there after I flush him, an' we'll find out where it is, an'—we'll go through his dump th' first time he gives us a chance. That bird's got somethin' on his mind an' he ain't th' sort that lays down. I believe him that far. He'll try an' put it across."

Jim grinned. "Maybe he'll take your message to Kelley."

Johnson frowned. "I reckon I hadn't ought to have said that, but—I was hot. Anyway, I guess if he does that cheap crook won't be surprised."

"Naturally," I put in, "he'll know you'll probably have him trailed. He's a man of evident education. It shows in his speech. He uses his brains."

"I'll say he does," Johnson sighed. "But—it looks to me like the best bet just th' same. Just for that I'm bettin' he'll lay low to-day an' drift out on that business of his, whatever it is, to-night. Want to go along with me if he does? If you do, drop in here after dinner."

We accepted the invitation and left.

"That's good police stuff," Jim grumbled as we walked back toward the office. "But I'm bettin' right now it will flivver. That guy talks about as much like a college graduate as like a gunman or thief. Son, this here is gettin' a little bit more mixed up all th' time. I can't see where he fits to save my life. Well, do we go spill this new dope to Semi or what?"

"The former, I guess," I replied. "In a sense, Jim, we're his outside ears and eyes."

"Not that he seems to need 'em, but I reckon we are," he assented. "It's a good deal like shootin' quail. He shoots his bird an' we retrieve it. Well—we'll carry this one back."

Consequently, instead of stopping at the office, we went straight up to the roof, to find the man Jim had likened to the hunter engaged in the very prosaic occupation of removing faded roses from his bushes with a pair of pruning shears.

He turned to us, and I remembered that he crumbled some half dried petals in his fingers as he stood, so that they dropped in a pink and red shower and lay at his feet.

"Welcome," he said. "Do you come perhaps bearing new grain?"

"That depends." I fell in with his mood. "At least we bring something new with us."

He smiled slightly. "And who can tell of the harvest until the Eternal Thresher has winnowed the wheat from the chaff? Yet the soul of man is like my roses. One must prune them to make them bloom, and man's soul blooms best perchance when life is not too easy, when his path runs not between roses, but through the midst of brambles set with thorns. Ease spells sloth, deterioration. Man and the soul of man grows strong through breasting storms, through adversities overcome. Tell me."

I did so briefly.

"A Uranian type if one is to judge by his physical attributes and his personal actions. The Uranian is explosive, in a measure prone to keep his own counsel, however, and do unexpected things."

"Like tryin' to call on a man via a fire escape at one o'clock at night," said Bryce.

"Exactly," Dual returned. "Such being the case, I am inclined to believe his introduction at this time completes Dorien's chart."

"Dorien's?" I exclaimed.

"Precisely. Recall that I stated in the beginning that one of his enemies was of a Uranian type?"

Bryce chuckled. "By granny! Well—I guess this chap would fit that description all right. I don't reckon he was tryin' to put over any Romeo stunt on that fire escape balcony last night."

"Scarcely," said Semi. "Wherefore we have now concrete individuals as well as symbols of them with which to work."

"An' things ought to begin to move?" Bryce suggested.

"To move," said Semi Dual. "Ah, yes, Mr. Bryce. And we shall await therefore what moves these individuals make, a little longer, I think, ere we make any move ourselves."

"Oh, sure," Jim agreed, "if you say so. But we thought we ought to tell you."

"You did right," Dual assured him. "Let me know each detail of what you learn. In the drama of life one must watch the action closely in order to understand."

"Drama of life," Jim grumbled after we had reached the office. "Well—with Venus an' Neptune, an' all th' rest an' now this Uranian bloke, we've sure got a fine collection of stars. Son—I'm goin' to lunch."

He was as good as his word, too, and I followed suit after running through my mail. Nothing more happened that morning nor throughout the earlier part of the afternoon until nearly four o'clock. Then Danny called up on the phone.

"Say, Mr. Glace," he began, "I gotta take a note over to Roma's sweety to-night an' place it in his lily hand."

"Dorien?" I interrupted, not as much surprised as I might have been, I confess, since it was scarcely more than to be expected that Miss Temple would have tried to communicate with him after her visit to the jail.

"Yes. But hold on! Somethin' happened this mornin'. A feller blows in an' asks for her, an' pretty soon she goes out with him, before I got a chance to give her Mr. Dual's message, an' when she comes back she looks all in. I goes up then an' gives her that note an' tells her th' rest of it after she'd read it, an' for a minute she looked awful funny an' then she says:

" 'Thank you, Danny—I—can't talk now,' just like that, an' I takes th' tip an' blows. Then this afternoon she rings an' asks me to get this note over to Dorien an' see that he gets it myself. Well, that's all, but I wanted to tell you an' ask you to tell Mr. Dual. I'll take th' thing over about eight. How's Mr. Jim?"

"All right," I said. "He's in his room. Want to talk to him?"

"Nope—but you tell 'im hot dawg things is sizzlin' an' th' worst is yet to come. S'-long."

As a matter of fact, I buzzed for Bryce as soon as Danny had cut off, and told him what the girl at the Kenton had done.

"Natural," he commented when I had finished. "Natural as goose oil, son. She don't want to go to Dorien herself 'count of Kelley, an' she figgers Danny's th' safest messenger she could get. Now if us an' Johnson can turn up somethin' this evenin'."

I nodded. "Yes—if we can."

"You don't seem all fired hopeful." Bryce grinned.

"Well," I returned, "if that chap's actually an ex-convict, as Johnson thinks, he won't be apt to leave very much around his room."

Jim shrugged. "Still—there's always that thing about a criminal's makin' a slip to go on. I've seen it work out more'n once."

So, too, had I. I telephoned Dan's latest report up to Dual, and devoted myself to routine things. Then Jim and I had dinner at a near-by café and went over to the station about eight.

Johnson was there before us, and we sat and talked till near nine. He had an address to which Willie was said to have gone after his release, and the rest, of course, was mere chance plus possible deduction on Johnson's part. Close to nine events, as it happened, proved him right. His telephone rang, and he answered, spoke briefly, hung up and reached for his hat.

"Come along," he remarked as he rose. "He's gone out not ten minutes ago, an' I got a car outside."

We left the station together and piled into the machine. He gave the driver directions and we were off. Ten minutes more brought us to a corner where we stopped.

"Walk from here," he said, and led the way around the corner and down a block of rooming houses of the cheapest sort. Midway of the row he turned and mounted a flight of wooden steps.

There was no bell in sight. He struck a match, found the button to one side of the door, and set his finger to it.

Presently the door was opened by a blowzy woman in a somewhat soiled and faded cotton dress.

"Good evenin'," Johnson began. "You got a man stoppin' here "bout six feet, with a heavy jaw, an' wearin' a brown suit?"

"Why"—the woman eyed him—"that might be Mr. Willie."

"That's right," Johnson said. "It is. Ain't home, is he?"

"No, sir—he went out a little while ago—"

"That's good, because I want to go through his room when he ain't inside it." Johnson flipped back his coat and showed his badge.

"Why—why—" the woman stammered. "Why—what's he been doin'?" Suspicion waked suddenly in her eyes, not unmixed with a vague sort of dread, I fancied.

"What did he tell you he was doin'?" Johnson asked.

"Why—he said he came East on business, though—it has struck me funny his goin' out so much at nights."

"Well—you take us up to his room, an' keep still about it, too," the inspector cautioned.

"Yes, sir." She turned toward a flight of stairs.

We followed her up. At the top she paused and opened a door and stepped back. "This is his."

"All right." Johnson stalked inside and snapped on a single incandescent that dangled from the ceiling on a cord. The sudden radiance showed a cheap room, a cheap complement of bureau, bed and two chairs. There was a stationary wash bowl beneath a faucet in one corner and little else, till he stooped and drew a traveling case from beneath the bed.

It was of plain leather, unmarked by any initial, and it wasn't even locked. He grunted as he wrenched it open and displayed some evidently new shirts, a suit of underwear ditto, some collars, and handkerchiefs and socks.

Abandoning it with a scowl of dissatisfaction, he attacked the drawers of the bureau, drawing them out and thrusting them back, and finding them empty save for a railway folder, a more or less crumpled collection of half a dozen neckties and some soiled clothing evidently waiting for the wash.

A rather battered raincoat hung on a nail driven into the inside of the door, to do service as a hook. Johnson seized upon it and literally turned it inside out. It yielded nothing, and he grunted for the second time as he replaced it:

"Beat us to it. Old hand all right. Knew we'd trail him an' probably frisk his dump. Foxy."

Bryce nodded. "Registered here as Willie, too. Do you reckon that's really his name by any chance?"

Johnson regarded him in a momentary silence before he snorted. "No, I don't. Nobody'd be darned fool enough to give a kid a name like that."

"It would be a low down trick, I'm admittin'," Jim retorted. "Reckon this bird has a sense of humor, all right."

"Humor?" Johnson was palpably laboring under a considerable degree of disappointment at scoring a complete failure in so far as any definite information about Weary Willie, so called, was concerned. "Maybe you call it humor, but I call it pretty slick. He's slick, all right, Bryce."

"Well, here," I said. I had picked the railway folder out of the top drawer of the bureau, because it had occurred to me that the man was reported from the West, and there was just an off chance that I might stumble upon some slightly illuminating mark. People do sometimes mark a station or something on that sort of thing when running them over. And while I didn't discover what I thought I might, I did get something none the less. The folder was that of a transcontinental system of railways, and on one margin was a name and address scrawled in pencil. I read it and held it out.

Hubert Kornung, 1022 Harrison Avenue.

Johnson grabbed it from my fingers and scowled again above it. "That's Kornung's number, all right," he announced. "It's just a block and a half this side of Park Drive. Well—say, how about it—what made him leave his address lyin' around, do you suppose?"

"I suppose he simply overlooked it," I suggested.

"Like I done, eh?" Johnson shrugged. "Well—maybe you're right. Anyway, he knows Kornung—or meant to see him. That much is plain, I guess. Let's get out." He flung the folder back into the drawer and closed it, shut the suit case and thrust it back under the bed.

We went back down the stairs and found the woman waiting in the lower hall in uneasy fashion, to judge by her manner and face.

"See here." Johnson resumed his questions. "You say that man came from th' West—any idea what part?"

"Why—no, sir," she said slowly. "But—I did get an idea it might have been from Utah, or Idaho, or Nevada, or New Mexico or Arizona—"

"Hold on!" he interrupted. "This ain't a geography lesson. Never mind namin' th' map. He didn't tell you nothin' definite? Take care, now."

"No, sir. I'm tellin' you th' truth. But—" she brightened visibly as at a sudden thought.

"But what?" he demanded sharply.

"Why, what made me think that was he did say he was an

engineer—not th' kind that runs engines, but th' sort that builds things—a—a—constructin' engineer, I think it was he said."

"Hell!" Johnson just about snarled while I glanced at Bryce and read comprehension in his eyes.

"Come on," he said, "we're done here," and led the way outside. And there he broke out again in a tone gone actually thick.

"Constructin' engineer! He's an engineer, an' so is Kornung—he's a consultin' engineer, an' this bird comes from th' West—an' writes down his address on a railway folder—"

"An' leaves it layin' around, because he didn't think it was worth a cuss to us," Bryce interrupted. "If he's what he told that dame he is, it wouldn't be, of course—an' naturally he wouldn't be hep to this mob's tryin' anything out on Kornung."

Johnson swore again with feeling. "I don't know whether he would be or not. Either there ain't no connection between our job and his at all, or—somebody's pretty deep."

Abruptly Bryce chuckled. "That's what you said this mornin' just before he told you there was a hole in th' bottom of th' sea. I been wonderin' all day if maybe he didn't mean that it was th' sort of hole that didn't—leak."

Johnson gave him a glance of supreme disgust. "Go on an' wonder," he said gruffly. "I don't guess it will hurt you to any great extent, an' it sure ain't doin' us any good."

CHAPTER X

THEORIES AND CONJECTURES

BUT IF JOHNSON was disgusted then, he was in little better humor the next morning around ten, at which time he came stalking into the office, and slumped into a chair without so much as a preliminary word of greeting.

"Where's Jim?" he growled.

"In his room," I said, and pressed the buzzer to bring him to what was plainly to be a further conference. "What have you on your mind?"

"Nothin'," he informed me shortly. "Not a thing. I ain't even sure I got a mind. Hello—" as Bryce came in. "Say—talk about your deep uns. That Willie guy is actin' mighty queer for any sort of engineer. Where do you suppose he was last night when we was goin' through his room?"

"I reckon you know th' answer?" Jim sat down.

"Part of it, anyway," Johnson rasped. "He was over pokin' around Kornung's house."

"My aunt," said Jim in genuine surprise. "He's worse than a crop of boils, ain't he?—always breakin' out in a fresh place. Was he tryin' to get in a window or crawl down a chimney or what?"

"He was tryin' to see somethin' without being seen, from th' way he acted," Johnson returned. "But—do you see what he done? I had two men on him yesterday afternoon—one to trail him if he went out, one to report to me at th' station if th' coast was clear. An'—he slips one of them by wanderin' half over town an' then heads for Kornung's an' goes to snoopin' around."

"Which," said Jim, "ain't no way to treat a consultin' engineer."

"Oh, dry up!" our visitor snapped. "An' listen—as it happens he gets over to Kornung's right behind that girl."

"You mean she went over there?" I questioned.

"In a taxi." He nodded. "Cool as you please. Tells it to wait, I guess, since it waited, an' goes inside an' stays till between ten an' eleven an' comes out an' drives back to th' hotel. Well, this night bird shows up on foot just about th' time she gets there, but my man didn't pay much attention to him till right after she'd gone in, when he sees him sneak up to a window where there was a light, an' try to peep over th' sash. After that he watches him close, of course. But he don't do a thing till th' girl comes out, an' then he takes himself off. My man manages to get a good look at him, though, an' it's th' same guy—no doubt about it."

"I don't reckon there was." All at once Bryce sat forward. "An' even if a hole in th' sea don't leak, I guess maybe a dictaphone or a telephone made into one does. Say—listen yourself till I check this up. Remember what Kelley told this girl about havin' her watched?"

"By Joey th' Poke?" Johnson suggested. "Say—that cheap purse snatcher—"

"Joey th' Poke nothin'!" Jim cut him short. "Just how many kinds of a fool do you think that mob master is? He'd tell her who was watchin' her, wouldn't he? Well, he wouldn't—an' if she went to see Kornung last night at his house, things is comin' on in that direction—an' I guess Willie was on th' job."

"Well—by Gawd!" Johnson stammered, as he caught the drift of Bryce's words. "An'—wait—that's how he knew so darned well which was Dorien's window—night before last. He's—been there before—when they was workin' on him. That settles it, I guess. He's Kelley's man—an' he's got his orders not to let that girl get in too deep. Lord!"—his eyes widened—"maybe that's what happened—maybe Dorien went too far an'—this bird butted in. She'd deny she knew him, of course."

"He'd hardly be perched on a fire escape at ten o'clock in the morning, would he?" I objected.

"Well," said Johnson slowly, "we don't know just when he was actually shot."

"Dual says ten was the right time, however," I pointed out.

Jim scowled. "An' he says Dorien's in love with th' girl. I don't guess he got shot that way, not—through th' sort of love he's talkin' about."

There was almost a plaintive note of realization as to the full bearing of his assertion, in his voice.

Johnson, however, had still a further suggestion to offer: "Well, say Dual's right. Maybe this chap was the man who was to pull off the whole play. He's a Western type, all right, an' old enough to show as her father, burstin' in after she'd been with Dorien all night. Say, there wasn't nothin' wrong—Dorien's about th' type to fight back when he found out he'd been framed, an' you can't tell what happened after that, maybe he pulled a gun or somethin' himself. We wouldn't hear of it, of course. Willie's just th' man to beat him to th' draw if that sort of shindy started—an'—I'll bet 'most anything he did."

He paused, breathing deeply, a light of dawning conviction on his face, and I honestly at that moment felt a similar conviction growing stronger in my breast. Willie was, as he said, of the type and age to have played the part—he had apparently known exactly where Dorien's suite was placed. Kelley had admitted a shadow of his own kept over Roma Temple to protect her from overt injury in her work. It checked with surprising ease, or seemed to.

And then Bryce cut in with a question: "Then how did Kelley get his arm broke?"

"I don't know, and I don't care how he got his arm broke," Johnson rejoined with some heat. "What I'm tryin' to do is get somethin' on him an' his mob. What do you think, Glace?"

"As a matter of fact, it sounds a good deal to me as though there might be something in it," I confessed.

"An' if there is, then maybe that was where th' girl saved Dorien's life, like Dual said she did," Jim swung completely over on another tack.

"Say—which side of the fence are you on, anyway?" Johnson demanded with increasing good nature.

"I ain't on any side," Bryce protested. "I'm just tryin' to dope this out same as yourself. It's just possible Willie saw red after th' gunplay broke an' kept on shootin', an' she interfered after th' third shot without Dorien's bein' killed. That would have saved his life, wouldn't it? Dual said it was her influence saved him—an' if she persuaded Willie to lay off after his man was down—"

"Oh, I getchu," Johnson cut short a further exposition of Jim's views. "Th' next thing is to prove it. An'"—he got up—"I've a notion th' best play is to give 'em plenty of rope on this Kornung deal, an' watch 'em close. Anyway, that's how I'm goin' to play it—"

The telephone interrupted with its buzz. I put out a hand and drew it to me and answered: "Yes—Glace speaking."

"Of Glace & Bryce?" came back a masculine voice.

I assented and stiffened in a sheer reflex of surprise at the response:

"This is J.H. Dorien, Mr. Glace. You will recall that you spent an hour in my quarters day before yesterday afternoon, perhaps."

"Perfectly," I answered.

"Could you make it convenient to call on me again, say, this afternoon?"

"Quite." My surprise was growing by leaps and bounds, but I tried to keep it from showing in my voice.

"Then, if you will do so, I will explain my purpose in making the request."

"Very well," I agreed, and hung up.

Then I glanced at my companions and gave them the information. "That was Dorien speaking. He wants to see Jim and me this afternoon."

"Dorien?" Johnson repeated as though scarcely able to credit his ears. "Good Lord—you don't suppose he's—goin' to— talk?"

"It's presumable, at least," I said, "that he intends to say something in view of what he'd done."

"That note!" Jim hit the end of the desk with his fist. His manner was one of excitement. "Dollars to doughnuts, Johnson, that's it. You expected her to tip him off about this Willie, didn't you? Well, she done it. Danny took a billydoo over there for her last night, an' he calls us up this mornin'. Oh, Pip!"

I nodded. I fancied he was right. "Furthermore," I said, "she saw us with you in Willie's cell, and she knows we called on Dorien—saw us there also, in fact. Quite naturally then she believes we're working with the police, rather than with any one else, as Dorien hinted when we were there before, and they know the police are aware something happened so far as his being shot is concerned, because you went to see him yourself."

"Yes, darn it," Johnson grumbled. "An' at that rate about all he wants is to tell you to lay off again like he did me, or to find out what you're up to."

"Or what you know about Willie," Bryce took up the business of conjecture. "Maybe she asked him to do somethin' like this in her note. An' if he's in love with her, he'd do it, of course. That's th' way with us masculine mutts. They can't come right out an' ask us, but if they can get Dorien to find out about what we think—"

"Hold on!" Johnson shook his head. "That might be all right, only I've got Willie placed as Kelley's man. She'd warn Dorien all right, but I don't guess she'd ask him to help furnish dope for her mob."

"Unless she was tryin' to keep herself out of any more of a mess," Jim persisted. "Anyway, I got an idea he's doin' it for th' girl. He didn't size up with me th' other afternoon as a man what you might call lackin' in nerve. I don't figure him as scared."

"Nope," Johnson agreed, "he ain't that sort. Just as a man, he strikes me as a pretty good sport. An' I don't know but maybe you're right about th' girl. If he's really fell for her as hard as you think, naturally he don't want her dragged around through th' courts an' th' press. See here—if there was some way of doin' it without that, I wonder if he'd be averse to trimmin' Kelley if he could?"

Jim considered. "Just for that," he said, "I wouldn't be above askin' him that very thing straight out this afternoon. He's askin' for th' interview this time."

"Lay off it," Johnson cautioned. "Right now they ain't any more certain of us than we are of them-not as much, to tell th' truth, because they don't know we're wise that they're playin' Kornung. But if Dorien gets hep to anything much an' should leak to that skirt—"

"Oh, cat!" Jim grumbled. "Th' other day Dual said this thing was wheels within wheels, an' as usual he's right. Ain't it th' devil that when it comes to a girl, a man don't know enough to take care of himself? They call 'em th' fair sex, but it oughter be th' unfair sex—for they do take advantage of us. It was a wise guy said a she-male was a lot deadlier than her brother; but—I bet he was a whole lot older when he said it than he was when he got the bump that made him say it."

"Oh, shut up!" Johnson admonished. "You clatter like a load of junk." Once more they were at their continual sparring.

So I interposed: "Don't you think you two are a good deal like the chap who got a letter and spent a long time wondering who had sent it, instead of opening it to find out? Perhaps after we get over to Monks Hall this afternoon we'll learn what Dorien wants."

Johnson grinned a trifle. "Well, yes," he assented, "I guess maybe you're right. Let me know if it's important."

"Quite naturally," he agreed; and he walked out.

"But see here—" Bryce began.

"Oh, shut up!" I said very much as Johnson had said before me. Jim was the best fellow in the world, but he loved to theorize and talk his thoughts aloud, and sometimes a man can think best alone.

And he seemed to understand, too, because instead of taking offense he chuckled, stuck a cigar in his mouth, and went back to his own room.

That left me to study the sorry, indeed what seemed the sordid, tangle out of which—as Dual said—had come the romance between Roma Temple and Dorien, a thing born out of cross purposes, conflicting actions, and emotions, yet fated to be should they ever come together, if there was anything in his science of the stars. And I knew there was, because I had seen him prove the verity of his calculations in which they were the integral elements too many times.

And he had said, too, that a field might lie barren and still grow fallow, later to bring forth a harvest when watered by honest tears. That would be tears of repentance, I thought. And he had asked who would give a hungry child or a woman in trouble a stone. That hinted even of the woman of Magdala—though, of course, it would seem that in Roma Temple's case there was no such error to atone. Yet—she had apparently done in the past a great many things she should certainly not have done, lending herself to the purposes of a man such as Archer Kell, who had preyed with her aid on wealthy men whose too susceptible heads she had turned.

Here, too, most certainly Dual had proved far from wrong in his assertion that she was a woman who had deliberately used her personal charms for material gain, only to be trapped in her own trap—to find herself not the snarer, but the snared, caught, held fast, overwhelmed with her intended victim in the end.

I harked back to Semi's remarks concerning fate, and his quoted lines:

> "And all unconsciously shape every act
> And bend each wandering step to this one end—"

It had been like that I thought with Roma Temple and Dorien. Each had gone the way—apparently of personal election—only to come together and strike fire like flint on steel, through the unexpected means of a blackmailing scheme in which she was to have been the seductive charmer, he the charmed.

And yet, according to Dual, that very thing had been foreshadowed in their separate births, led up to, drawn near to, actually brought about in due season by the steady, immutable progress of the stars. Fate, indeed. But it was strange how Dorien, leading the life of the man about town outside his hours of business, footloose in a sense at least, not bound by any too exact code of morals, and Roma Temple, adventuress, since that was what one practically had to call her, using her God-given graces to betray men through their baser natures, had finally met and looked into each other's eyes and read a greater meaning into life than they had ever known.

Yesterday Dual had said that Weary Willie completed Dorien's chart. And I knew enough to know that in such a thing one would expect to find each of the planetary bodies or stars. And I knew vaguely the attributes assigned to each star at least.

All at once I smiled. He had named Jupiter and Venus, the Moon, Neptune, Saturn and Uranus, had mentioned the Sun in Dorien's chart and Roma Temple's—had said they were in trine, a favorable aspect to each other. He had mentioned Mercury and Mars. He had said that now he had assigned an individual to each planetary body for which it stood as a symbol. And he was watching—how they moved, and thereby predicating the actions of each one. And of them all it seemed to me that probably Kelley was of the more martial type—one who threatened violence—might even have tried to accomplish it the other night through the agency of Willie. Here, too, then Venus would seem to be in conflict with the purposes of Mars. An opposing Venus truly, as Jim had said, at that rate.

I looked at my watch and rose. It was past twelve. I walked across to his room and went in.

He glanced up and grinned. "Son," he said, "if Solomon had three hundred wives an' a thousand chickens, what's the least common divisor of the average man's affections for one woman?"

I laughed. "I don't know," I declared. "I'm no Solomon and my own particular affections have never been to any great extent divided."

"Neither do I," He got up and put on his hat. "Let's go ask Dorien."

CHAPTER XI

ANOTHER CALL ON DORIEN

WE HAD LUNCH at a near-by café and turned into Monks Hall a little after one.

This time there was no difficulty about gaining Dorien's presence. Quite evidently we were expected.

"Misser Glace, Misser Bryce, yessir," Kato murmured as he took our hats. "You sit down, please. Misser Dorien have lunch."

We took the seats he gave us and he withdrew through a door in which Dorien himself immediately appeared. "Join me, gentlemen?" he invited. "Fix you up in a jiffy if you like."

"No, thanks, we lunched before we came over," I explained, eying the man. Since I had seen him first, he seemed to have improved in a physical way, as was evidenced by the fact that he now was moving about.

"Just so," he said and came forward to his chair. "This is good of you, considering that on the occasion of your former visit I was scarcely cordial—especially toward the last."

He smiled slightly as he took his seat, not merely with his lips, but with a little twinkle in his eyes.

"Well—not exactly," Jim said dryly.

Dorien laughed. "As a matter of fact, Mr. Bryce, I hadn't exactly placed you at that time, and—"

"Now you have?" Bryce interrupted.

"At least, I know you are working with the police."

"And not with Kelley?"

Dorien set his lips. "It isn't much use for us to argue, is it?" he returned after a moment of hesitation. "Well, let us admit, then, that friend Kelley has seen fit to recently take an interest in my affairs—"

"Particularly night before last," Jim pressed what might be almost called an attack.

Dorien frowned. "You mean the man on the fire escape, of course. Frankly, I don't know whether there was any connection between them or not."

"But Miss Roamer thinks so?" I put in a word.

"Miss Roamer?" he repeated.

"Or Miss Temple. See here, Mr. Dorien, you assume that we're connected with the police because she saw us in this man's cell with Johnson yesterday morning."

"Naturally." He smiled again the least bit.

"And has communicated with you since."

He looked slightly startled as he saw where I had led him. And then he shrugged. "Honestly," he said, "I'm sorry you people have got hold of this affair at all. We should have greatly preferred to have settled it between ourselves."

"You an' her an' Kelley?" said Bryce.

Dorien actually winced. "As I just said, Mr. Bryce, I'm sorry you've seen fit to interfere," he returned. "At the risk of seeming both unreasonable and stubborn, I'm going to refuse to discuss what's past and done. It *is* done and my interest is altogether with the future."

"Very well," I said, as he paused. "That being the case, just why did you ask us to come here?"

He answered me quickly enough, too. "Simply to ask you to cease your activities in this matter in so far as Miss Roamer and I are concerned."

"You appear to prefer the name of Roamer," I shot back, and watched him.

"Why not?" he snapped in somewhat heated fashion. "It's

her own as it happens—Muriel Roamer. You might as well have all of it since you've managed to get part. And I don't intend to have it dragged around through your filthy courts."

Apparently Johnson had been right in his assertion that Dorien's actual purpose had been to ask us to lay down our hand and quit. He had said as much and he sat there now before me, lips compressed, lids a bit narrowed, cheeks a trifle flushed. I waited a moment after he had delivered what he seemed to consider a final declaration of his purpose, and then I tried a different tack.

"A commendable determination, Mr. Dorien, and one which I think justifies the assumption that you feel more than a casual interest in Miss Roamer—that you entertain, let us say, a genuine affection for her."

"A *genuine* affection." He met both my regard and my suggestion with a challenging light in his eyes. "It's none of your business, really, but—I'm not inclined to deny it, Mr. Glace."

"And—are we to further assume that you have reason to think your affection returned?"

He set his lips again before he answered. "I have *every* reason to think so—every reason in the world."

"In spite of the fact that Kelley used her to frame you?" Bryce broke in before I had formed a reply.

Dorien came halfway out of his chair with a jerk. "Damn you—I've asked you to drop that!" he rasped in a voice gone thick with irritation. "Now listen. Muriel Roamer is the girl I expect to marry—the girl I love. And I don't give a curse what she's done before I loved her. And I've told her that, and I've told her I wasn't any spotless lily myself. She knows, and I know. We understand each other. It's our business, I take it. Why can't you drop it?"

"Mainly, because we don't want you bumped off some balmy evening, an' this bunch seems pretty active in that direction," Bryce said.

"Oh, that?" Dorien's lips curled. He sank back in his chair with a somewhat unsteady breath. "Piffle—man! I can take care of myself. Of course, I realize that you're doing your duty as you see it. But I can't help you. The cost would be too great. See here—I'll tell you something: Muriel Roamer is largely responsible for the fact that I'm alive, and she's altogether responsible for my having a mighty different viewpoint on life.

"I was pretty near dead for quite a while, and I did a lot of thinking. But—I won't go into that. I don't give a damn for Kelley or his gangsters. Get 'em any way you can, if you want to, but—leave her and me out of it. Gentlemen—she's a girl—and—she wants to do what's right. You'd understand a lot better if I could tell you what I know—but—well—put yourself in my place—I can't."

Actually, I rather admired him as he sat there appealing as one could hardly doubt for the welfare of the woman he frankly announced he loved.

"In a sense, Mr. Dorien," I said, "we seem to be working at cross purposes. Technically, my partner and I are not even connected with the police. Now let's put the cards on the table instead of playing them quite so close to our chests."

"Oh, I know," he smiled in somewhat mechanical fashion.

"You're an independent firm. I looked you up. But you're working with Johnson, and—he seems a persistent chap. His idea to send you over to see me when I wouldn't talk to him, I suppose?"

"It was his idea that we might be able to help him break up a blackmailing organization," I replied. "Johnson is a sincere official who tries to do his duty and he is rather tired of seeing this sort of thing put over under his nose. Now in view of your attitude toward Miss Roamer, I presume it is your desire to assist and protect her in any way you can."

He nodded quickly. "Absolutely."

"Then you'd better watch Kelley." Jim spoke for the first time in minutes. "I'm shootin' it straight, Dorien. He wants her himself an' he ain't th' sort to lay down a whip when he's got one."

"A whip?" Dorien leaned forward. "Just what do you mean, Mr. Bryce?"

"You," Jim told him flatly. "You gotta look this thing straight in th' eye, Dorien. Just sittin' tight an' holdin' your jaw ain't goin' to get you out of the woods by a long shot. She's a valuable asset to Kelley, besides bein' th' woman he wants, an' means to have— an' anybody he thinks is in his way is apt to get hurt a lot worse than you did once."

For possibly thirty seconds Dorien made no response. I saw him clench a hand slowly.

"That's your assumption," he said somewhat hoarsely at last.

"I'll lay you a bet it's a mighty good one," said Bryce. "An' here's somethin' that ain't one at all. He's havin' her watched every move she makes. She ain't been to see you since we was here before, has she?"

Dorien breathed deeply. "If you know that—you're having her watched yourselves."

"Well—that's our business." Bryce shrugged. "We're watchin' everybody pretty much. That ain't th' point. Dorien—that mutt's usin' you as a club."

"Using—me?" The man's eyes widened.

"Sure. Put it up to yourself. You're in love. Why else did she nearly faint yesterday mornin' at th' jail when she found out where th' man we had there was grabbed. That's common sense, ain't it, provided she cares for you like you think? An' I ain't castin' any doubts on her love for you, either. I'm provin' it, I guess."

"But—my God! This is awful!" Dorien got up. He was shaken, I could see it—shaken in his innermost being.

He began to pace back and forth, his face furrowed by the emotion Jim's words had waked. And suddenly he turned back to stand before us with set jaws between which his voice came gritting.

"I suppose I understand you—that he's threatening me—dogging her—turning her days and nights into hell, and I suppose I can't prevent it, but—if he touches her—if he harms her—I'll get him—I'll get him if it's the last action of my life."

"Yes-s," Jim made almost drawling comment, "an' it's just something like that we're tryin' among other things to prevent. There's been enough powder burnt in this thing already."

"Then—why tell me about it? Do you think I've got red ink in my veins or what? What are you getting at?" Dorien's lips drew back, exposing teeth in the sort of wolf snarl of a fighter, straining to the attack.

And Bryce nodded. "Nope—I ain't questionin' th' redness of your blood, Mr. Dorien," he returned. "I reckon it runs just about man normal. I reckon you wouldn't balk breakin' Kelley or any other man what touched her, with your hands. Well—that's th' sort of man I like. One what won't fight for his woman's a pretty stinkin' sort of skunk.

"But—what I'm gettin' at is this. We—Glace here an' me, an' Johnson, an' th' department are ready at any time to back up that sort, against men of Kelley's type. We're standin' out all the time for real men; an' folks who are tryin' to clean themselves. Now don't misunderstand me—but that little girl has made some mistakes, which ain't no sign she hasn't a right to come clear any time she wants. That's up to her, but—if she wants to, why—we're mighty ready to help. Most folks has got a wrong notion of th' police, but I've been on th' force myself, an'—takin' 'em far an' by—th' men what try to take care of you while you sleep are a pretty decent sort."

"Oh—darn it all, I know it!" Dorien sat down and took his head in his hands. Presently he looked up. He was a trifle more himself.

"Gentlemen," he began. "It's a pretty rotten mess. The mere fact that I was shot doesn't matter. I got about what I deserved for things I've done in the past. But the real point is this. We want to come clean as Bryce puts it—to make a fresh start and it wouldn't be a very good start, would it, if we began it in the courts, with all this stuff we both know of advertised?"

"Personally, though, you ain't wastin' any love on Kelley?" said Jim.

Dorien smiled a bit wanly. "I am not."

"Then listen to this. He's usin' you as a club, like I told you. I'll lay you any odds on that. Now you call her up an' tell her you understand the situation an' that you'll take care of yourself, an' if Kelley gets you he'll have to be a good deal smarter than he is. Then you do what you promise—"

"I'm not worrying about myself," Dorien interrupted.

"I know you ain't," Jim assented quickly. "But—she is. You tell her you'll be all right an' tell her not to do any more of Kelley's work."

"Oh, but that's utterly foolish. She wouldn't," Dorien broke out.

"Not unless she was forced to," Bryce amended.

"By Kelley, you mean?" Dorien fixed him with his eyes.

He nodded. "Kelley, sure. Has she worked for any one else?"

"No. And—" Dorien paused.

"And what?" Jim prompted. "See here, man, we're your friends and hers."

"He trapped her into the first deal years ago, damn him!" Dorien literally spat out the oath.

"Then you do what we say—tell her you'll take care of yourself. That 'll help her a lot."

"I'll do it." Dorien rose again to his feet. "I'll do it. This hasn't been the sort of talk I expected, but—I'm glad we've had it."

"So are we," I assured him, rising also, while Bryce got to his feet. "I think we understand each other better than we did at the start, no, but what we have felt all along is that your main purpose was to escape without any unpleasant notoriety or fuss. And—" On impulse I added: "I think I can promise you some such ending of the matter." As a matter of fact, whenever he could do so, that was how Semi Dual worked.

He met me halfway at once. "If you can accomplish that, you'll make us both your debtors for life, Mr. Glace."

"In the meantime," I said, "let us know if anything of interest turns up."

"I'll do it—I will, really." He put out his hand.

I took it and Jim followed suit. Our departure was vastly different from the occasion of our former call, and I felt that our time had not been wasted, even if we had accomplished no more than that. What Jim thought I didn't know, but he had quite evidently played for the same object.

For the rest of it, he burst out as soon as we were in the street: "Snappy—dippy—he's nuts on the subject of that skirt. Kelley tricked her into th' game she's been playin'. That's what she's told him. She wouldn't do nothin' more like it. Then how about this Kornung stuff?"

"Ask Kelley," I retorted. "You suggested she might be forced into helping him yourself."

"I'd like to," Bryce grumbled. "I'd like nothin' better."

I changed the subject. "Was it wise to tell Dorien she was being watched. He'll tell her, of course, and—"

"She won't leak," he said with sudden conviction. "Honest, son, she won't. I ain't copperin' those two on a bet. An', anyway, ain't Semi tryin' to get her to him, an' when he does you don't reckon he's going to entertain her with any polite conversation, do you? Nope—he's goin' to show her what she's into without blinders, an' then show her a way out. Right now is Kelley's inning, but wait till Dual goes to bat. Personally, I never cared to mix it with a woman, an' when Semi an' that little blond love bird get on th' job, you watch Mr. Kelley take to earth. Well, we've settled one thing this afternoon. Those two are crazy about each other, in spite of each one knowing what th' other is. An' there you are. Didn't Dual say Dorien was likely to see th' best in her, an' take her into his house?"

"Exactly," I assented.

"An' when a man marries, that's what he generally does."

"Admitting all that," I said, "there doesn't seem any marked indication of Dual's getting in touch with her yet. I rather thought his note would hit her where she lived."

"She's chewin' on it," Bryce rejoined. "She don't know him like we do an' she's figurin' on whether or not to take a chance. Gosh—if you started to make a fool out of a guy an' found that th' bigger fool he was th' more you loved him, wouldn't you wonder just where you was comin' out?"

"Probably," I told him, smiling. He seemed to have summed it up in his characteristic fashion.

"An' didn't he just about tell her by what he told Dan to say that if she wanted to know what he knew she'd have to come after it herself?"

I nodded. "Just about."

"Well, then," he went on with an air of satisfaction. "All we've got to do is wait. He's playin' this game of star roulette."

Star roulette. It wasn't a bad designation of Dual's astrological symbols and circles, his recently voiced assertion that this present matter was an affair of wheels within wheels.

I laughed. "Star roulette, Jim," I said, "is pretty good."

He chuckled. "Except that for him it don't seem to be no

gamble. An' th' best thing we can do is to wait till he says where th' marble drops."

I nodded again. Things seemed pretty much at an impasse and I had nothing better to suggest.

CHAPTER XII

ANOTHER SURPRISE

BUT THOUGH WE couldn't see it, the various forces involved in the affair were moving—or to carry out Jim's simile a bit farther, one might say that the wheel was going round. Semi himself sometimes used that very expression, alluding thereby to the march of events, the ceaseless whirl of the so-called zodiacal circle, first plotted by the ancients in the days of a misty past—the eternal turning of the Cosmos itself.

Still there was little enough to indicate the march of events on the surface as we descended from a car, threaded our way to the doors of the Urania Building intent on reaching our offices only, and encountered Roma Temple face to face.

I saw her first, and knew that she saw us by her eyes. They lighted with what I might possibly best describe as a latent smile and then, as they met mine, the thing spread to her lips.

"Good afternoon, gentlemen," she said, pausing and thereby bringing us both to a halt. "I've just been up to see your very strange friend on the roof—a wonderful man in a—most unusual place."

"Er—yes," Jim croaked, plainly taken aback by the frankness of her words.

Her smile deepened. She positively dimpled for an instant. Unless I was mistaken she enjoyed the effect she had produced. The consideration shaped my own response.

"Quite so, Miss Roamer—and we have just returned from

calling upon your friend, Dorien, at Monks Hall. A somewhat vicarious exchange of visits, is it not?"

It shook her. I could see she had not looked for any such verbal or actual tit for tat. And then—she laughed softly. "Jack? Why—don't you let him alone, Mr. Glace? He won't talk unless he wants to, really." And abruptly there was a challenge in her smile.

"But you see, Miss Roamer, that's it. He sent for us," I said, and watched her little, almost unnoticeable, start of surprise. Frankly I found myself attracted to her, despite what I knew of her past. There was an intangible feminine magnetism about her, like an aura, indescribable, of course, but none the less to be felt.

"Jack sent for you," she repeated. "Did he also tell you my name was Roamer, Mr. Glace?"

I laughed back at her then. "Inadvertently, yes."

She set her lips. Rather unconsciously as it seemed to me she turned her head and looked back down the length of the foyer toward the bank of elevators.

"You're clever, Mr. Glace—and your friend is a man who reads the human heart, I think. Are you using merely your brains in what you're doing, or—his?"

The question was a facer. How much had Semi deemed fit to tell her? I asked myself. And before I could answer Jim solved the problem.

"Both," he blurted out. "He don't only read hearts, Miss Roamer—he reads stars. I reckon you went up to ask him how things was comin' out?"

She narrowed her lids. "You're not a fool, whatever you are, Mr. Bryce," she said slowly. "I—I never dreamed that Danny was your agent—and his. I was fooled completely."

Jim gasped. She knew—even about Dan. And then he rose to unusual heights. "Well—you know, Miss Roamer, they say 'a little child shall lead 'em.' That's out of th' Bible, an'—it's God Almighty's truth."

She gave him a startled look. "Why—I've heard it—of course. Gentlemen, good evening."

She turned and lost herself in the sidewalk crowd.

"My aunt—she knows th' whole bloomin' business!" Jim pretty nearly groaned.

"If she does, Dual told her himself," I suggested.

"Huh?" He stared. "Well, that's right, I guess. Come along." He led the way to an upgoing cage.

Johnson was with Danny in my private office. It seemed to be getting a habit, so far as the former was concerned, and it was not any great shock to find Dan after our recent meeting with Roma Temple.

Plainly they had been talking, but broke off as we came in. And then Dan grinned.

"Hello," he announced. "I just been tellin' Johnson that skirt had come through at last an' gone up to see Mr. Dual. She couldn't keep away after she found out he knew somethin' till she found out what it was. So I took her up there an' turned her over to him, an' beat it back an' shucked my uniform. She darned near balked, though, when she saw where he lived—an' read that stuff he's got on th' plate that rings th' chimes."

I nodded. I could imagine the effect of the words etched in a glass inlay on the annunciator plate at the head of the bronze and marble stairs, on any one approaching Dual's peculiar abode in the woman's frame of mind. They had given me a shock myself the first time I ever saw them, and I was merely a reporter trying to cover an assignment to interview him at the time.

> Pause and consider, oh, stranger. For he who cometh against me with evil intent, shall live to rue it, until the uttermost part of his debt shall have been paid; yet he who cometh in peace, and with a pure heart, shall surely find that which he shall seek.

"So you're done at the Kenton?" I said.

"Yep." Danny ducked his head and sighed. "He said, once I got her to him, I was to quit. I guess he thinks he can handle her from now on himself."

Johnson fidgeted in his chair. "But it's a cinch she'll get wise that Dan was planted there to steer her, if she don't find him when she gets back."

"Oh—she knows that already," I told him, and explained about our meeting with the girl herself.

He scowled. "But—good Lord, how'd he explain leadin' her into that sort of a trap? What do you suppose he told her?"

"The truth," said Bryce almost brusquely. "That's all he ever uses. He's th' only man I ever met what could fool you that way, but he does. An' she's wise to the fact that he done it. You could see it in her eyes. He's made her feel he was on th' level in gettin' her up there, no matter how he did it."

"She's a wise bunch of goods," said Johnson.

And Jim protested. "I don't care how wise she is, he shook her. A wise one ain't no different from th' others when they're in trouble."

Johnson nodded. "Well," he confessed, "he *has* got a way with him, I'll admit. Did Dorien talk?"

"To some extent." I dismissed Dan, who went with evident reluctance, and told the inspector of our visit to Monks Hall.

"Wanted you to lay off, eh?" he grunted. "Well, I doped it about right. Says th' girl's name is Roamer? Well, maybe it is. It sure looks like them two had been shootin' straight with each other here of late. Sort of funny, ain't it?"

Bryce lighted a cigar. "It is an' it ain't. It's funny th' way you mean it, an' th' other way it's not. I reckon this hurts 'em about as much as it does other folks—especially as it ain't on record that either of them ever thought very much of th' love stuff to date."

"Nope," Johnson conceded. "But I did not come over here to talk about that. You know this here Weary Willie? On th' level, that guy's gettin' on my nerves. I can't make him—I simply can't make him, boys."

"No?" I said. "But I thought this morning you had him pretty well placed as Kelley's man, and possibly the chap who shot Dorien the night this whole works started."

"So I did," he told me, frowning. "But that was this morning, and this afternoon what does he do but pack his bag, grab a taxi, and drive over to Kornung's house an' walk in like a man come to pay a visit!"

"He did that?" Bryce questioned as Johnson came to a rather dramatic pause.

"Just that," the inspector reaffirmed. "Sends off th' cab and walks up an' rings th' bell an' goes inside. He was still there at last reports. Now, if he's Kelley's man—what th' devil is th' notion?"

"An' if he's a construction engineer an' Kornung's a consultin' ditto—why, maybe he's come to consult him," said Bryce with a speculative expression on his face.

"Then, what was he doin' on Dorien's fire-escape?" Johnson demanded, scowling at the very point he raised.

"I don't—know." Jim considered it slowly, while I found myself baffled no less than my two companions. "But—wait a mo! Didn't you say Kornung had done a lot of work in the West before he located here?"

"I said I understood he had," Johnson agreed.

"An' Weary Willie gave his residence th' other night as 'out West.' Now, where's th' connection?"

"Blessed if I know," Johnson sighed. And yet his tone lacked conviction.

"But—it's there. They know each other or—did," Jim declared. "By granny, there is something in it, I tell you."

"What?" said Johnson.

"Enough to make him go to Kornung's house."

"After he sneaked around it last night, while that girl was

inside? Back up, Jim—you're forgettin' that, I reckon. Nope—I tell you there's some sort of stall in this whole business—an' what I'm worryin' about is whether or not there's somethin' comin' off?"

"Coming off?" I repeated.

"Sure," Johnson nodded. "We don't know what's been going on so far as Kornung is concerned till th' last few days, mainly because we ain't watched that end of the play before, an'—as Jim says, this Willie is from th' West, an' looks th' part. Now, I don't just know how th' game is bein' worked, but I ain't over-lookin' Kelley—or th' fact that Willie's th' man who may have fell down in tryin' to frame Dorien, either. What's to prevent his bein' th' man picked to make Kornung pungle up?"

"But," Bryce questioned, "why plant him in Kornung's house?"

"I'm guessin'," Johnson said, "just guessin', but—suppose he is from th' West. Suppose he even may have known Kornung out there, an' then he comes here an' stops with him, an' gets next to the girl—wouldn't that make it easier to make th' deal stick if he claims to know her or be related to her?"

"Great cat!" Jim exclaimed. "Ain't that pullin' it pretty fine? Where'd Kelley pick up a man that knew Hubert Kornung?"

"Maybe he didn't. Maybe he just got a name Kornung knew an' is passin' this man off as somebody Kornung did know really. You know he's been here in town for quite a number of years. It wouldn't be so hard to do it. This bunch is trained to throw a bluff."

"An' th' girl's goin' through with it?" said Bryce.

"Sure she's going through. Ain't she been over to Kornung's an' had dinner with him in a private room, both th' last few days?" Johnson seemed to feel he was clinching a point.

But Jim demurred. "I don't believe it. I don't believe she's givin' Dorien th' double cross."

"Dorien?" Johnson retorted.

"Yes, Dorien." Jim flushed slightly, but stood his ground.

"I—dang it, I may be a fool, but I've got a sort of boneheaded faith in that little skirt's stand with that gink."

"Oh, bunk!" Johnson grinned. "I got more faith in Kelley's hold on her than I have in that sort of lovey-dovey mush. Didn't he tell her what to expect if she kept goin' to see her sweety? An' don't you suppose she knows that guy well enough to know he's apt to keep his word—an' don't she know where we caught Weary Willie—didn't I tell her myself an' pretty near knock her off her feet? Wake up, Jim; you're on your back."

I smiled. My partner had surprised me more or less. I began to wonder if he, too, had come under that utterly feminine and subtly fascinating and magnetic something that seemed to cling about the girl we had met on our way up. Certainly his expression of faith in her integrity of purpose with the man who had declared his faith in her love had been forcible enough.

"Your idea bein' that she's goin' through with Kornung as a safety on Dorien's life," he remarked.

"That, an' her share of th' jack, of course."

Jim shook his head. "Dorien's got plenty of th' last. She's doin' this because she's afraid of Kelley where he's concerned. Well—what are you plannin' to do at that rate?"

"Watch," Johnson told him. "I'm goin' to have a man on Kornung's place every night, till something breaks or don't—"

Suddenly he laughed. "Lord," he said, "if anybody could hear us talkin'—they'd think us a fine bunch of tecs, I guess; but it's a relief all th' same to sort of talk a thing out—even if you ain't doin' more than guessin'. An' that seems to be about all we can do as yet on what this mob's up to right now. There's so little blame to take hold of. They don't give us any real cause to make a move. They're too slick for that."

He rose heavily to his feet. "Well—so-long, boys." He jerked his chin upward. "Nothin' new from th' man on th' roof, I suppose?"

"Nothin' except that he seems to have connected with the

girl like he set out to," said Bryce. "I'd have liked to been in on their conversation."

"So would I," Johnson agreed. "Well, so-long." He walked out.

"I sure would have liked to been in on that," Jim said again when he had disappeared. "Dan says his place up there jolted her, an' I reckon it did—an' I reckon he jolted her worse himself. She's a wise little jane, I don't doubt, but she wasn't wise enough to expect to find a man in a white an' purple dressin' gown, in a garden on top of a roof. I'd have liked to have heard what they said."

"Naturally," I assented. "I felt the same way myself."

What, I wondered, had gone on between Semi Dual and the girl who had squandered the first years of her youth and womanhood and beauty in playing upon the weaknesses of men, when she had come into his quiet, inscrutable presence? Danny had said she seemed shaken. But—what had she felt and what had she said—and how far had Semi made her understand his motives and ours? How far had he succeeded in convincing her that in this newer ambition of hers to forsake the life she had been living, he and we stood her friends? Surely a long way, I thought, since when she met us she had smiled—and there had been a suppressed and yet eager something, I fancied, lurking within her eyes.

"What do you think of Johnson's latest attempt to get all the pieces into this puzzle picture?" I asked.

Jim shrugged. "It looks all right on its face. That's the trouble with this thing—there's so darned many ways th' pieces look like they ought to fit—an' of course only one of 'em is right."

"Which one?" I smiled.

Jim grinned. "I'm bettin' it's th' one we haven't thought of yet."

I laughed. It was like him to say that, and yet—one guess was as good as another. He might be right. Even Dual, who, as Muriel Roamer said, read hearts—he, with his quiet understanding of human nature, its weaknesses and strengths, its hopes and ambitions and foibles, its grandeur of endeavor, its sorrow of mistakes—had made no definite move, save in bringing her to him—save in collecting what data he and we could gain to apply to what he had spoken of as "the harvest." The harvest! What sort of a harvest? I asked myself. As a man sowed so should he reap. It was an old saying, but the truth. I had seen it proved.

It was the thing on which hinged, as it were, Dual's preachments of a law of immutable justice meting out the measure of cause and effect on good and bad alike. What a man sowed—and surely at that rate, for some of those involved in the present issue, the harvest must be a harvest of wrath.

And as though to prove that in so much at least I was right in my estimation of already known values, the man we knew as Weary Willie was shot down that night, at Hubert Kornung's house.

CHAPTER XIII

A JOLT FOR JOHNSON

I READ IT the next morning as I sat at breakfast. It glared back at me from the printed sheet:

PROWLER SHOOTS FRIEND
OF HUBERT KORNUNG

W. Willie—a civil engineer from the West, who is stopping with Hubert Kornung, a consulting engineer, at his residence, 1022 Harrison Avenue, was shot by an unidentified man, believed to have been a burglar, just after he and Kornung had driven into the garage in the rear of Mr. Kornung's residence about eleven thirty last night.

Mr. Willie and Mr. Kornung had taken dinner down town and later gone to a theater. Returning home they drove the machine into the garage, and got out. Mr. Kornung says he first noticed the man who shot Mr. Willie lurking in the shadows close to the garage door, and spoke to him, asking him what he wanted. The reply was a command of "Hands up!"

Kornung, being armed, immediately opened fire, and in the ensuing interchange of shots, amounting from all accounts to a genuine fusilade, Mr. Willie was struck by a ball which pierced his left shoulder and knocked him to the floor of the garage.

Mr. Kornung believes that he wounded their assailant, but if so, not severely enough to prevent his escape. Just how the affair might have terminated indeed is an open question, except that city detective B. Lezner, who chanced to be in the neighborhood, was attracted by the shots and ran to the rescue, shouting.

The gunman, hearing his shouts and realizing that he was in danger of being trapped, instantly fled, colliding with Lezner near the garage door and hurling his weapon into Lezner's face, staggering him and thereby making his escape.

Upon recovering from the blow of the gun, and realizing that his man had fled, Lezner ran on into the garage, where he discovered Kornung assisting Mr. Willie to a sitting position. Kornung himself had sustained a slight wound—a mere graze on one cheek—but was otherwise unhurt. It is his theory that the man was hiding in the garage intent on burglarizing the residence later that night. He can think of no other reason for his presence since there was nothing of value in the garage except a couple of spare tires.

Mr. Willie was removed to a hospital, where he was resting easy and in no immediate danger at last reports. At headquarters the affair is regarded as but one more example of the unfortunate wave of lawlessness which seems to be sweeping the country at this time.

I laid down the paper and pushed back my plate and rose. Weary Willie had been shot. So much the story told me. I discounted the rest of the account, because I felt sure that Johnson had seen to it that it was carefully colored to suit his own fancy in the matter before it had been given to the press, as witness the assertion that a city detective had "happened" to be in the neighborhood instead of actually watching Kornung's house.

Consequently my whole desire was to get in touch with Johnson and Bryce and learn what had actually occurred.

And, as if the wish had been father to its realization, the telephone rang as I went to get my hat.

I answered it, and Johnson's voice came back:

"Hello, Glace. Get over to the station on the jump. Seen the papers?"

I replied in the affirmative.

"Well, we flivvered it, but it was a near thing at that," he went on. "Anyway, the net's out for Kelley an' we'll get him. I've just finished talkin' to Bryce."

"I'll be right down," I said, and hung up with a tight sensation gripping my every nerve.

Kelley! Was it possible, I asked myself, that Kelley had been mixed up in this second shooting? Apparently he had. He might even have been the gunman in Kornung's garage, from the way Johnson talked. But—it was a rather surprising thought. I went out and caught a car down town and made my way to police headquarters.

I found Jim already there with Johnson in the detectives' room.

The latter nodded as I came in. "What did I tell you?" he said. "This just about cinches it, I guess. Talk about your clear, cold blooded nerve."

"What really happened?" I asked as I took a chair.

"There was plenty happened," he said gruffly. "We'd have caught our bird right on th' ground, too, if Lezner hadn't been blinded when he threw his gun in his face. But he got a slant at him, for all that. It was Kelley right enough."

"The man in the garage?" I questioned. The thing was true, then.

"Yes." Johnson scowled. "We got his gun, an' it's th' same caliber as th' one Dorien was shot with. What gets me is why he was there at all, with this Willie person on th' job, an' th' girl already in th' house."

"The—girl!" I stammered in surprise.

His lips twitched. "Oh, yes—I was forgettin' you don't know about that; but along last night she goes over there, walks up an' pulls out a latchkey an' lets herself inside. You can see about how far things must have got between her an' Kornung by that, I guess.

"Remember what I suggested yesterday might be back of Willie havin' gone over there, bag an' baggage, like he did? Well, she goes in, an' she didn't come out till after th' shooting occurred. Then she runs out right at th' last. Lezner says he saw her just as he ran around the house, an' right after she shows up at th' garage an' asks what's th' matter, like she had the right— an' Kornung tells her to go back inside."

"Kornung did?" I repeated.

"Yes. Looks like even then he wasn't hep to th' whole thing's being a plant— an' of course, things havin' foozled, Willie don't spill any information. Kornung an' Lezner helped him inside, an' Lezner telephoned in what had happened as soon as they'd called an ambulance. I went over, of course. Kornung hadn't much to say, an' th' girl looked sort of funny when she seen me; but never let out a word, except to tell Kornung she'd like to see him some time to-day. Right after that she blows. Kornung really seems to think Kelley was just an ordinary thug, an' that Lezner saved him an' Willie from bein' worse shot up than they was. He guv me a check for our police fund to show his ap- preciation. Looked like he was pretty well upset, so I didn't tell him th' worst." He chuckled.

"But you're sure it was Kelley?" I persisted.

"I ain't. Lezner is," Johnson returned. "But look at it. Willie is his man so far as we can dope it out and the girl was there in the house between eleven an' twelve o'clock. I seen her right after twelve myself."

"But—why shoot Willie?" Bryce queried.

Johnson eyed him in pitying fashion. "Accident, of course. Komung tipped over th' beans when he started shooting, after Kelley told him hands up. Th' gun that hit Lezner was empty when he picked it up. I reckon that's what saved his life. I called Kornung up a little while ago and told him I wanted to see him. Then I called you an' Glace. Thought maybe you'd like to go along."

"You're right about that, anyway," said Jim.

"Well, come along."

We went out to a police machine which put us down after a quick run to Kornung's house.

We went up to its doors and Johnson punched the bell. Komung answered the ring himself.

"Come in, gentlemen," he invited, "I was watching for you. In here, if you please."

He led the way into a reception room opening off the front hall and gave us chairs.

He was very much indeed as Johnson had described him days before, with heavy forehead, wide and thin-lipped mouth, somewhat stooped. To-day there was a slight wound, little more than an abrasion of the skin on his left cheek—so slight a thing indeed that he had apparently not even taken the trouble to have it dressed.

"All I wanted," Johnson began, "was to see if things looked any different to you to-day than they did last night."

"Why, no, inspector," Kornung smiled in a somewhat deprecating fashion. "I'm afraid they do not. In fact, I hardly see how they could. You see, the thing was extremely sudden. We drove into the garage—I'd left the doors open when we started down town right after six—and we got out of the machine, and I was reaching over to turn off the lights when I noticed this fellow crouching back in a comer as though trying to escape observation and spoke to him as I told you. You already know the rest. I had a gun in my pocket—always carry one, in fact. I reached for it as I spoke to him, and when he replied with a demand that we put up our hands, I fired the first shot, firing purposely over his head. After that things were pretty breezy for possibly a minute. He ducked back of the machine—or I'm sure I'd have got him."

"I wish you had," Johnson declared with a force that made it quite evident the words came from his heart. "You still think he was hiding there in order to get into the house later?"

"What else?" Kornung asked. "Either that or he meant to steal the car. That seems rather far fetched, since he must have known we'd have to drive it in beside him first."

Johnson nodded. "Rather. Now this man Willie—last night you said he was a civil engineer."

"He is." Kornung inclined his head. "Actually, I don't know him very well, but—frequently men of his profession come to see me—because of my own profession and—well, if there is much to talk over I have them out to the house rather than at a hotel. It saves time in discussing any matter in hand, as well as avoiding interruptions such as come up at an office."

"He's from the West?" Bryce cut in quickly.

"Yes. Nevada." Kornung turned his head as he replied. "He has done work for the State for quite a number of years—or so he says. I have no reason, however, to doubt his statement. He apparently knows his business."

"No, I suppose not," Jim sighed.

I looked at Johnson and found him frowning. Kornung's reply seemed to have proved unexpectedly frank to both my partner and him.

There came a momentary silence and then Kornung spoke again. "Isn't it possible, inspector, that the man actually tried to burglarize the place and went into the garage to wait after he found somebody up and around?"

"Meanin' the young lady who was here last night?" Johnson caught him up quickly.

"Yes. Miss Temple. She came over to see me and decided to wait when she learned I was out. You heard her tell me she wished to see me sometime to-day, I think."

"Yes," said Johnson rather blankly, and then as though deciding to force the issue: "You've known her long?"

"Roma?" Kornung's thin lips relaxed to a smile of reminiscence, and firmed again as he frowned. "As a matter of fact, inspector, I've known her since she was a child—and her father before her. At one time he and I were by way of being pals. I can't see how it can bear at all on last night's occurrence, but—you'll understand her presence better if I tell you that for several years she actually lived in my house.

"Recently I have seen little of her. She—like so many of the younger generation—has gone her own way the last few years, and unfortunately that way has not been wholly one of which I could approve. Still, there has been no breach sufficient to bar her from coming to me any time she wished to consult a friend."

"Yes, yes—just so. I understand."

Johnson's tone was suddenly somewhat husky. I felt I could imagine about what was in his mind. If Kornung had known Roma as he called her since childhood, what then became of Johnson's laboriously built-up explanation of a blackmailing plant engineered by Kelley to fleece the man.

"Well, I guess that's all. Sorry to have took up your time," he went on and rose.

"Not at all—not at all," Kornung rose also as did Jim and I. "Sorry not to have been able to help you myself, inspector. But you have so little to go on, to tell the truth. I'm not even positive that I hit the man—though last evening I fancied I had. I'm not a bad shot as a rule. But—if I can be of any assistance—don't hesitate to call on me at any time."

"Thanks," said Johnson almost shortly, and we got ourselves outside.

"Can you beat it? *Can* you beat it?" he began as soon as we were in the machine. I couldn't blame him, either. Our interview had certainly ended in a way far from what we had expected.

"I ain't tryin' to beat it," Jim made an equally gloomy rejoinder. "What I'm tryin' to do is figure where we get off. If he's known th' girl since she was a kid, Kelley never used her to frame him. Maybe Lezner was seein' things last night."

Johnson scowled. "Lezner's a pretty cool-headed boy, old man."

"I ain't sayin' he ain't." Jim refused to argue the point. "But did you notice what Kornung said—that she was goin' her own way, of which he didn't approve? Migosh—he might as well have said he knew what she'd been doin', an' then he says she could come to him if she needed a friend, an' here's this Dorien

trouble. That may explain her goin' to see him th' last few days—
an' even her havin' a latch key to his house. If she lived with
him, like he said, she probably had one, and she probably kept
it when she moved. At that rate he knows Kelley most likely
an' he had as good a chance to see him last night as Lezner did.
Then why would Kelley—"

"I'll tell you when Kelley's got," Johnson interrupted. "An',
see here, Jim, I'm tired of speculation. What I want now is facts.
Kornung knows th' girl all right. Willie is from the West—been
workin' for th' State—so Kornung says. Let it go for the present.
I'm goin' over to th' hospital now an' see what he says for himself."

He leaned forward and spoke to the police chauffeur, and
leaned back, frowning. "What I can't see is why your man Dual
don't get busy. So far, beyond tooling that girl up there to see
him, he hasn't made a move, an' it ain't th' way he generally
works."

Quite slowly Jim found a cigar and set it alight after several
attempts in the swiftly moving car

"Maybe," he said at last. His faith in Dual was no less than
mine as I knew and I suspected Johnson's final remark had not
been as well considered as would have been the case had the
man been less upset by recent events. "But"—Bryce puffed out
a mouthful of smoke—"if he ain't made any moves so far as we
can see to date, I'm willin' to lay you what you like it's because
it wasn't time or there wasn't any move to make. After we see
Weary Willie, th' sick engineer, suppose we go over an' give him
th' latest dope an' see what he says. That 'll give you a chance to
make any kicks you've got to his face."

"All right," Johnson assented and lapsed into a gloomy
silence, until the car stopped in front of the hospital doors.

CHAPTER XIV

SEMI DUAL ACTS

A NURSE LED us to the door of a room and ushered us into the presence of the man we had come to see. He was in bed, reclining on a back rest and turned his head as we entered, but gave no other sign of recognition until the girl had withdrawn.

"Good morning, gentlemen, I had hardly expected to meet you again so soon or in such guise, but—time makes changes in us all," he said then, and smiled with lips and eyes in a somewhat surprising fashion, considering the experience through which he had recently gone.

"'Mornin', Willie," Johnson returned. "Yep. I reckon it does. Last time you'd been tryin' to see a man what had been shot up an' now you seem to have stopped a bullet of your own."

"Oh, I didn't stop it," the man said, his smile widening. "It went clear through, and didn't do much harm. Sit down, gentlemen—there are chairs enough, I think." He turned his glance as though to verify the count.

We seated ourselves. Willie was still a puzzle to my mind. As before, he was speaking in the cultured accents of an educated man. And if I were any judge, he was laboring under some form of suppressed emotion—was amused by our call upon him, was almost facetious in his manner.

Johnson, however, plunged straight into a number of questions as soon as he was seated.

"See here, Willie, are you an engineer or ain't you?"

"I am, Mr. Johnson."

"From the West?"

"Yes, Mr. Johnson."

"Nevada?"

"Who told you that?"

"Kornung. We saw him this mornin'."

"Mr. Kornung was mistaken as to recent years. I have been in Nevada, but more recently in Utah."

"He says you've been working for the State."

Willie smiled again and his eyes appeared to twinkle. "That is correct."

"What sort of work was you doin'?"

"Road work—work on the State highways mostly."

"For how long?"

"Fifteen years."

At least Willie was talking at last and Johnson went straight ahead.

"What did you come East for?"

"To see Mr. Kornung."

"An'—Dorien?"

There came a pause. Willie's smile faded, and then he said slowly: "I admit I wished to see John Dorien, Mr. Johnson, but time—the same time I mentioned a moment ago, has altered that wish now."

"Just how?" Johnson's tone was pugnaciously suspicious.

Once more Willie smiled. "Frankly, sir, because in the interval I have learned what made an interview nonessential, and met—shall I say—a mutual friend?"

"Of yours an' his?"

"I trust so, and of yours, I think—a large man of very commanding presence and somewhat peculiar ways and rather ultra views—a man of great understanding and insight—of gray eyes, a slightly aquiline nose, a firm and yet, as I found it, compassionate mouth. He came to me this morning, wearing a soft gray suit, and a soft gray hat, and left me in a softened mood."

"Semi Dual!" The words were Jim's. He voiced them and glanced at Johnson, while his eyes widened and an actually exultant expression leaped into being on his face.

"That was the name he gave," said Willie. "Semi Dual—a peculiar name, which he explained to me by stating himself the son of a Persian father and a Russian mother. A most remarkable man, Mr. Johnson, whom one feels instinctively that he may trust."

Semi Dual. He had been here—inside this room, before us. He had come and talked with Willie and departed. I glanced at Johnson—who not twenty minutes before had complained because Semi was making no moves. And I found his heavy face a quandary—a thing of blended emotions, of surprise, of baffled understanding. And as he caught my eye, his lips began to move.

"Well, yes—he's a mighty strange man," he said, and I read a double meaning into his words. "So he's been here, an' after his visit you don't want to see Dorien any longer. What did he tell you?"

"Why, I think he told me the truth, Mr. Johnson. He said also that in his estimation you would call upon me, and that when you came it would hardly be needful for me to explain those points he and I had already discussed—that I should refer you to him, rather than further exert myself."

"Well—" Johnson began, and got up. The glances of the two men crossed. That of the man in the bed was clear, steady, re-enforced, as it occurred to me swiftly, by something Dual must have said. Johnson's was clouded, and he went on abruptly. "At that rate I'll ask you one more question and get out. What really happened at Kornung's last night?"

"You have seen the papers?" Willie asked.

"Yep," Johnson nodded.

"Their account is practically correct. I induced a nurse to let me see one."

Johnson frowned. His lips drew back slightly.

"Except that Kornung had a girl waitin' for him in his house. Did you know that?"

"A girl?" Willie contracted his brows slightly. "Who, may I ask—since it seems you think I ought to have known her?"

"Roma Temple, th' girl who was in Dorien's rooms when he was shot."

"Oh, Miss Temple," said Willie slowly. "But—Kornung has known her pretty much all her life."

And there it was. Johnson's face went red and then a sallow white. I saw him knot the fingers of one hand into the palm before he snapped another question.

"You know that? He's mentioned her to you?"

"Oh, yes."

"All right." Johnson turned toward the door.

We followed him out and down the hall and out to the machine.

"Urania," he snarled a direction, and flung himself back in his seat.

The car started with a jerk.

I glanced at Jim. The situation was tense, and he didn't help it a bit by the grin that wreathed itself on his lips and his following words:

"An' that's th' man you said wasn't movin'. Well, he seems to have had a talk with Willie an' then put a padlock on his mouth; an' that's more than we've done ourselves. Tells him to refer us to him— Oh, my aunt! An' did you notice Willie—he was actually jazzed up—you'd 'a' thought somebody'd left him a million dollars—an' your mention of Roma never feezed him— he knew Kornung knew her—"

"Oh, dry up!" Johnson interrupted. "He knows of her as Roma Temple, an' so does Kornung, an' she says her name is Muriel Roamer; tells Dorien it is, an' as good as admits it to you. Well— somebody lies—"

"Holy smoke!" Jim gasped.

"Jolts you, eh? Well—I thought maybe it would, since you hadn't seen it yourself," Johnson sneered. "But I noticed it when Kornung pulled it myself. You want to get over believin' what everybody says."

"Shut up, Jim," I prompted. There was no doubt that Johnson was in an irascible mood, despite the fact that Dual had finally done the very thing he had been complaining he had not.

Bryce accepted my suggestion, too, and held his tongue until the Urania was reached.

Still in silence we made our way inside and up to the sun bathed garden on the roof. It lay there inside its vine grown parapets a thing of beauty, an oasis of peace and quiet undreamed by the busy life of the world that throbbed and milled and ebbed and flowed beneath it in the streets.

And as we mounted the top of the stairs and the mellow chimes set its golden air aquiver, Jim nudged me with an elbow and gave vent to a low toned exclamation: "Look!"

But I had seen already—and so had Johnson. I heard him actually catch his breath.

Before us were man and woman—Roma Temple, Muriel Roamer, whatever her name might be; and Semi Dual, still clad in the modern raiment the man in the hospital had described. They had been walking among his roses, and—at the sound of our coming—they paused.

Semi Dual and the girl of the Kenton— the little opposing Venus, as Jim had called her—here side by side in his garden. It was the last thing I myself had expected, and yet I felt my heart leap to a quickened beating. Dual was moving—had moved, no matter what the police official beside me had said or thought. And—he would keep on moving. At last he had taken the ends of her tangled skein of life into his strong, sure hands. And he would hold them, unravel them strand by strand from now till the end of the need was reached.

"Come on," I said, and went toward them with Johnson and Bryce.

The girl's eyes were a trifle widened, her breath a trifle quickened, as shown by the rise and fall of her breast. Dual had given her a rose, and she held it in her fingers so that it lay against the soft fabric of her gown, above her heart, as red as a drop of its blood.

But Semi's tones were as inscrutably calm as ever as he spoke to us in greeting.

"Good morning. I think you know Miss Roamer. She rang me up this morning, and came over to see me and explain concerning her presence last night in Hubert Kornung's house."

She had done that—he had made it possible. Yet his telephone was not listed in the book. It was a private number, and—he had given it to her—provided for her need of calling him, should it arise. Oh, yes—he had moved since last we had seen him—moved far in advance of the rest of us. And the girl—she had come to tell him of her actions. Why? Had it been to show her good faith, to prove beyond any question that his faith in, his help of, her at this time was deserved? As I bowed in response to Semi's words, I fancied that it was.

"Oh, yes, I know Miss Roamer—or Miss Temple, as I've always known her till now," Johnson said, slightly stressing the surnames in a way of meaning Semi did not miss.

"Misapprehensions are so easily arrived at, are they not, inspector?" he responded. "Roamer, however, is correct. You may see how easily the given name by which in the past you have known her may be formed from the name by which you shall know her last."

"Oh, sure," Johnson nodded. "That's a common enough trick in aliases, I guess."

Dual was carrying a light stick, as was his custom when he elected to desert his quarters and walk abroad. He swept it in a half circle.

"For long," he said, "I have endeavored to cultivate an atmosphere of peace and calm—a restful eddy, as it were, in life's turmoil here within my garden; and I have succeeded, I think, save when some inharmonious life vibration is introduced from without. Should he who asks feel offense at the hand from which he receives, or appreciate rather the labor involved on the part of the one who gives?"

It was general enough, but Johnson got it. His face flushed deeply.

"I beg your pardon," he said in an acutely self-conscious fashion. "I'm upset, I admit."

Dual inclined his head. "And I appreciate both the fact, inspector, and the cause. You have visited the hospital this morning?"

Johnson nodded.

"And found I had been there before you—whereat you were both taken unawares and in a measure displeased."

"I wasn't expectin' it." Johnson was visibly embarrassed. "Up to now you'd appeared to be mainly interested in Miss Roamer, here, so far as I could judge."

"Wherein your judgment was mainly right." Dual glanced at the girl beside him. "For the simple reason that in my estimation a great deal of what has occurred since I have taken an interest in this matter at your solicitation, and of what must yet transpire before its termination, must needs revolve around her. Consequently I sought to bring her to me, and succeeded as she understands. In addition, I sought to win her confidence, and in that, too, I feel that I have succeeded—since I have proof in the fact that she called me up this morning, and that she is here."

"Indeed yes," she said impulsively as he paused.

"You understand, Mr. Johnson?" said Semi Dual.

"I guess so." Johnson didn't appear very positive about it right then.

"That she trusted me, and called me in order that I might not misunderstand her presence in Kornung's house last night— that I might feel my trust in her was in nowise misplaced—and, having called me, came up to explain in person."

Abruptly Johnson asked a question: "See here, Miss Roamer—does Kornung know that is your right name?"

"Why, certainly." Her regard did not falter under his.

"Then, why did he call you Roma Temple this morning?"

"Why"—she flushed, and then went pale—"possibly because he knew I was known by that name to you, if at all, Mr. Johnson. Generally he calls me—Muriel."

"An' Willie?"

She set her lips. "The man I saw—at the jail—the man who was—shot last night?"

"Yes—does he know your name is Roamer?"

"Just a moment, inspector," Dual interrupted. "If you will bear with my wishes in this matter I will undertake that the answers to most of the points you are raising will eventually appear. At present Miss Roamer and I are waiting for her companion, Mrs. Meese, whom we have summoned from the hotel."

"You've sent for her—you're bringin' her here?" This appeared to be Johnson's morning for surprises at the hand of the man he had alleged was doing little. "What for?"

Dual smiled. His eyes met those of the girl in what seemed a perfect understanding before he answered. "Because I deem it best that for the time being, and until this matter is finally concluded, Miss Roamer should disappear."

"Dis—appear?" Johnson faltered. His expression was actually dazed.

"Apparently. Perhaps we should qualify it to that extent," said Semi Dual.

The chimes cut in on his words. I turned my glance toward the head of the stairs. It fell on a woman something past middle age, to judge by her graying hair. She was coming toward us at a pace that bespoke an inward nervousness. And as she came nearer, she addressed Miss Roamer:

"Roma—what has happened now?"

"Nothing, Matilda," Muriel Roamer told her. "I want you to meet Mr. Semi Dual, of whom I have spoken to you. We are accepting Mr. Dual's hospitality for the next few days."

CHAPTER XV

A PREDICTION OF DEATH

SO THAT WAS it. For some inscrutable purpose of his own he wished the opposing Venus to disappear, and he brought her here to this garden of his with the woman who had been her companion when she posed at the Kenton as a Western heiress and sought to entrap Dorien.

It was a strange turn in the affair that had been holding my attention and Johnson's and Jim's for days—and yet, I felt, one which could be no more than the logical outcome of all else, at least in Semi's brain.

"And now," he said when the introductions had been extended to embrace me and my two companions, "let us go inside, if you please, in order that I may explain in so far as I may what has already transpired and what in my judgment may follow directly because of what has been."

Turning, he led us into the inner room and invited us to seats, taking his own accustomed place beside the great desk.

It was literally covered with papers, bearing the symbols of his work. I noted the fact—proof positive that whether or no he had made any tangible moves before to-day, he had not been idle. And I knew instinctively that it was of the results of his working, set down there in sign and symbol, that he was about to speak.

For a moment he seemed to mentally marshal his words before he began. "Man at the time of his first breath establishes the vibratory ratio of his atoms; wherefore man thereafter responds to cosmic vibration, each according to the basal ratio established at his birth. It is this that men call fate—that intangible force that seems to shape, and does shape in major measure, the character of the average person and consequently his acts. Some days ago I quoted the lines of a poem to my friends Glace and Bryce:

> "Two shall be born the whole wide world apart,
> And all unconsciously shape every act
> And bend each wandering step to this one end—
> That one day out of darkness they shall meet
> And read life's meaning in each other's eyes."

Beyond me Muriel Roamer caught her breath. I did not wonder—could imagine the meaning she read into his words.

Dual, however, gave no sign that he heard, as he went on: "The key to fate itself lies wrapped in the word *unconsciously*— in this—for so long as man unconsciously lives in the basal ratio of his atomic vibration, so long in the eternal scheme of the cosmos itself must his unconscious following of a basal keynote form his character and shape his course. And only when the soul of man awakens to his weaknesses and inevitably resulting dangers may he hope to defy his fate, using the force of a *conscious* spirit as a light to illumine an otherwise darkened path. Hence it is written that man is bound to the wheel, and that only through conscious understanding may he finally escape. All of which the present matter affords an excellent medium to illustrate."

He paused and swept his deep gray eyes about our little group.

"In what I am about to say, let no one take offense. I shall state the truth, kindly in so far as I may, but literally for the single reason that it is—the truth. Because of what I have already stated, John Dorien lived the life of a man about town for years. Because of it, Miss Roamer lent herself to his attempted ensnaring—through her very evident charms. And I have read my own figures erected to cover the time of his shooting—and of his birth date and hers—and mark you, so strong is this thing men call fate, that it was certain that should they ever meet, as shown in those very figures, they should read life's meaning in each other's eyes.

"Wherefore, having met, each found his life take on a different meaning—and she found herself involved in an inward struggle, wherein every higher impulse of her nature was whipped into sudden opposition, both to the initial purpose of their meeting and the life she had formerly led. Am I right in this, my child?"

"Yes—oh, yes." She was white to the lips. She rose and went toward the window, stood there looking out.

Dual followed her with his eyes, then brought them back to us. "And yesterday afternoon she gave me the birth date of her father—and of the man Archer Kell—"

"Kelley!" Johnson broke in. His irritation seemed to have vanished, though he was palpably still on edge.

"Yes, Mr. Johnson, and"—Dual gestured to the mass of papers on the desk—"I worked on those two problems through the night, and I learned that those men had also 'lived their atoms'—gone blindly, as it were, along life's path, wherefore fate shaped their steps in tune with cosmic vibration, and all unconsciously they had stumbled on, to the present moment, like those who walk in their sleep, with open but unseeing eyes. May I tell them, Muriel Roamer, what I have told you that I read?"

"Yes—do what you think best." She turned and came back slowly again to a seat beside Mrs. Meese on a couch against the farther wall.

"Yesterday, when first I met her," Semi resumed, "I told Miss Roamer of her father—that he was a man whose fate had been unkind—whereby she was thrown on the mercy of others at approximately ten years of age. And I told her that in so far as any moral characteristic of his own was concerned, that fate was undeserved. Yet no man lives to himself alone, and a man may be made or marred at times through his associates.

"And I told her further concerning the man known as Kelley—that in so far as she herself was concerned, his ratio of personal vibration was essentially evil as affecting hers. Toward her he was a malefic, to use a term of that study of the stars in which you know I believe. Yet Kelley came into his influence upon her when she was still of a formative age—at a time when she was easily strengthened or marred. What then happened? Some one has said that 'each man kills the thing he loves,' and so strange is fate at times that—we may find ourselves attracted to another, despite the fact that the following association prove as fatal as the luring flame to the moth. What happened then?"

"Let me tell it!" Suddenly Muriel Roamer cried out. "Let me tell it as I told you yesterday myself—in my own words."

She caught her breath and went on quickly.

"I—I never *wanted* to live the life I *have* led—I never meant to. I've hated it— loathed it at times—I've despised myself and my race. I—I was a girl when it started—and I met Archer Kell. He came to my guardian's house. I was living then with Mr. Kornung, who took me after my father's trouble came upon him, and kept me till five years ago—ten years. It was at that time Archer Kell came into my life. Oh—I'd seen him before— but—I spent a good deal of my time at school, and it was only after I had finished that he paid me any attention, really, when he came to Mr. Kornung's house."

"Kelley came there?" Johnson interrupted.

"Yes, Mr. Johnson."

"What for?"

"I don't know, really. But after I came home, he began coming to see me, until one night Mr. Kornung ordered him off, and told me he didn't approve of our association. At that time I wasn't very wise. I—I had learned to like him. I—I guess it was fate, as Mr. Dual says.

"I met him clandestinely at times, in tea rooms and such places. "That's how it all came about. One day he brought an acquaintance with him to such a meeting. I know that now, but then I thought it was only a chance occurrence. Later, I found out he was a married man. I swear I didn't know it then. How could I? I trusted Archer and I never dreamed the horror he had in mind, that—that—he was planning even then to use me to extort hush money from his alleged friend. It was only afterward—when he told me, laughing—that I was able to understand.

"But that is what he did. He engineered the whole thing until one day he arranged for this man to meet me and take me to a certain resort. Later he came there, and there was a horrid scene. The—the man paid and I never saw him again, but Mr. Kornung heard of it, and ordered me out of his home. I went to Kelley—there was no one else to whom I could turn. I told him he had wrecked my home and then—he told me what he had done—told me my reputation was destroyed—that he had meant to get me into his power.

"I—I lost my head, I think. I hadn't been trained to be self-supporting. He—he offered to take care of me if I would work with him. Even then it was not till later that I learned he was the head of a blackmailing gang—that there were other women, being used as I had been used, to prey on men. I agreed to what he proposed because I couldn't see anything else to do, and—after a time"—her face altered, hardened as it seemed—"after a time, I got to a place where it seemed to me that if men were so dreadfully foolish, they were actually bringing their fate upon themselves—deserved what they were getting. Oh, it's a horrible confession—and I know now how horribly wrong!"

Her voice quivered tensely and then died away.

Dual broke the ensuing silence. "Here, then, we see once more an illustration of the keynote operating, since in both Archer Kell's radical figure and that of Miss Roamer, were influences calculated strongly to bring such a thing about. Kell is of a martial nature, headstrong, impulsive at times, beneath the sway of strong emotion, yet even so of a calculating type, as witnessed by the fact already known to us that he did not hesitate to employ in his sordid scheming the woman who, could we ask him, he would doubtless declare he loved. For love like all else is dual in its manifestations, being both of the spirit and of the flesh. Yet herein was he killing the thing he loved—for wherein is there more certain death than in a spirit debauched—vandals may profane a shrine—and the slime of the world may besmirch a body—and what, my friends, does it matter, if the spirit remain untouched?

"And in this did his victim escape—that there dwelt within her a force, never quite overthrown by his debasing plottings, to flame into open rebellion and waken her spirit at last. Life, my friends, is a sea, an ocean of cosmic currents, on which men either sail or drift—and he who captains his soul may resist those currents and shape his course despite them, as a mariner steers his bark on an actual ocean by means of recognized stars."

"Stars?" said Jim, picking up the word as Semi paused.

Dual smiled. "Stars, yes, Mr. Bryce—they may serve to chart the way of a ship on the sea or the course of a human life—to order it, direct it, and prevent shipwreck on either material or spiritual rocks."

Jim nodded. "An' at that rate it would look as though th' way you've figured it, Dorien an' Kelley an' Miss Roamer here an' her father had been pretty much like folks driftin' on a raft."

"The comparison," said Dual, "is not inapt—drifting, yes—most certainly drifting, caught up, carried forward, spun this way and that by the currents of fate. And now let us look to the concrete example, having dwelt on the general considerations to this extent.

"In the figure I set up for Mr. Dorien's shooting, is shown a martial influence through which his injury was directly brought about."

"Martial?" Johnson interrupted. "You just said Kelley was of a martial type." His manner was somewhat excited as he made the point.

"Nor do I retract either statement." Dual met him with no least hesitation. "Upon them I am perfectly ready to base a further opinion that it was Archer Kell indeed who fired the shots, while under the stress of some intense emotion which put him in a killing rage."

"Is that straight, Miss Roamer?" Johnson turned to the girl on the couch.

She nodded. "Yes—oh, yes—Archer shot him—and— all the while—I was trying to hold his arm and begging him to quit. He was like a madman."

"You was holdin' his arm?" said Johnson while there flashed through my mind Dual's assertion that she had largely saved Dorien's life. "Well, I guess that explains his not shootin' very straight. But—how did he break his arm? You didn't do that, did you?"

"No." She shook her head. "I was trying to stop him, and Mr. Dorien's Japanese servant—"

"Kato!" Jim broke in. "Well—by granny, Dorien offered to have him jujutsu us th' first time we went to see him."

Miss Roamer eyed him. "He grabbed Archer's arm and twisted it some way, and I heard the bone snap. It—was awful!" A shudder shook her.

"Whereby," Dual resumed, "it is once more demonstrated that in Miss Reamer's presence, as shown by the planetary positions in the figure of the shooting, Dorien's life was both imperiled and saved at one and the same time. It was through their reading regardless of known results that I was led to declare that it was largely because of her he is still alive.

"After that we knew the main details of what occurred. Dorien was taken to a hospital. Kelley's arm was put in a cast. Miss Roamer devoted her time more or less between the two men, until such time as it was certain Dorien would live and Archer Kell had recovered from the fracture and was getting about. It was at about that time that the man giving his name as Willie appeared on the scene—a man shown as an enemy in Mr. Dorien's radical figure, and needs be, as he is, of a Uranian type. This man, as we all know, was arrested outside his window, and Miss Roamer was asked to confront him at the jail by Mr. Johnson, in an endeavor to determine whether or not he was connected with Archer Kell—as I may state now, he was not."

"He ain't Kelley's man?" Johnson sat up and stared.

"No, Mr. Johnson. As a matter of fact, he has every reason to be one of his bitterest enemies rather than his agent."

"Then, I reckon that's why Kelley shot him. He knew he was stayin' with Kornung an' he laid to get him."

"Kelley—do you mean it was Kelley— last night," Muriel Roamer faltered. "Mr. Johnson—are you sure—"

"Dead sure," he well-nigh shouted. "An' I've got him where I want him now. Kornung was right about his hidin' in th' garage to pull off somethin' later, even if he didn't know what it was. He was wise Kornung and Willie were out in th' car an' he figured he could pot his man at short range. Well, wait till we get him an' we'll sweat him."

He smiled a trifle grimly. "You know, Miss Roamer, all I been tryin' to do is get somethin' on that dirty crook an' bust up his gang. An' this time he's guv me enough to do it. I'm glad Kornung missed him—on th' level, I am." He leaned back and sighed like a man contented.

"And yet," said Semi Dual in a tone half musing, "I will make you a prediction, Mr. Johnson, that what you promise so sincerely will never be brought about by yourself."

"No?" Johnson challenged the suggestion. "You mean we won't catch him or what? You mean he's got a chance to escape with a general alarm out for him—"

"By no means," said Semi Dual. "For no matter how general your alarm may be, inspector—there is a greater, a more potent menace directed against him from which there is no escape.

Archer Kell, like a man caught in an irresistible current, is drifting swiftly toward a physical dissolution."

I stiffened. It was a death sentence his lips were pronouncing. I looked at Bryce and found him puffing out his stubby brown mustache.

I heard Muriel Roamer gasp.

"You mean he'll be—killed?" said Johnson, his voice gone suddenly husky.

"Killed—probably yes," Dual said calmly. "Because of his own acts. Because both his luminaries are afflicted by both his malefics in his natal chart. Because he has lived his life unconsciously as I have pointed out. Hence, since he has done naught to change the vibratory ratio of his natal polarization, he must inevitably respond at this time to the cosmic vibrations which shall bring about his death. For it is so that a measure of a man's existence is written in the hour of his birth."

CHAPTER XVI

A REVELATION

FOR A TIME there was an almost breathless silence and then Johnson asked a further question.

"How?"

"What does it matter?" Dual responded gravely. "Let the cosmos answer, Mr. Johnson, since it is a cosmic debt he pays—the score of a lifetime squandered—given over to noxious deeds. And to you a word before I go further into this matter. I called at the hospital this morning and spoke with the man I found there, and cautioned him to refer you to me when you came, as I felt you would, chiefly because my study of all the data in my possession had convinced me of a truth which he himself confirmed, and I did not wish at this time to have you take independent action on any information you might obtain.

"In the beginning I told you this matter would, as you may remember, be involved—a thing of cross currents—cross purposes—and in that I was right beyond doubt."

He paused briefly and again went on: "We are arrived now at a point in its progress where we are facing a pregnant situation, from which, as I firmly believe, justice upon the guilty will be born, even though long deferred. Do you understand?"

"No, I don't," said Johnson baldly, "except that you had a good reason, accordin' to your way of lookin' at this thing."

"That," Dual accepted, "is sufficient. What did you learn at the hospital?!"

Johnson told him. "Why—that he'd been workin' for th' State of Utah mainly on th' State highways for fifteen years."

Semi nodded. "That was correct in a sense, the technical truth—the letter of it if not the spirit. He might have added, however, that he did his work as a man convicted of murder— that during those fifteen years he was a convict under an inde- terminate sentence which the State Board of Pardons eventu- ally saw fit to terminate."

"Huh!" Johnson actually grunted.

At another time I would have smiled. There was a sort of grim humor in the man's declaration that he had been working for the State. But I did not smile right then. I kept my eyes on Dual.

"Well—my Lord!" Johnson rumbled. "That explains it. Th' other day at the jail I felt sure he'd done time somewhere all right. You say murder."

"Yes, Mr. Johnson, but a murder he did not commit."

An inarticulate sound drew my glance around to Miss Roamer. She was sitting rigidly upright and she scarcely seemed to breathe.

And then Dual addressed her. "Muriel—come here, my child."

She rose and went toward him slowly, like one moving in a daze.

He, too, rose and placed his hands on her shoulders.

"Muriel—Roamer—lift up your heart, for a great joy is about to come upon you—Julian Roamer—your father—is a free man, and though last night he stood in a deadly peril through you and his love for you—he will live."

Julian Roamer! I felt my senses whirl. Julian Roamer—the man of the fire escape—the man in the hospital bed: Muriel Roamer's father! Of all the unexpected developments, this was the most gripping. Wheels within wheels and where shall their course run out? Dual had said.

"Willie!" I heard Bryce mumble.

And then the girl's voice—tense as the quivering string of a violin:

"Oh—my God!"

And then Muriel Roamer, that man's daughter standing before the strong man who gripped her shoulders, gripping his arms with tightly clinging fingers, stared up into his face to read its truth.

"My—father," she spoke again. And—I didn't—know him—I looked into his eyes and—denied him. Did he know me—did he *know* me—*did* he?"

Dual answered gently: "Aye, Muriel, he knew you, but he would not say so—because of John Dorian."

She shrank as from a whip.

"He thought—" she said, and drew back, releasing her hold of Semi's arms. "He—thought—that—"

"He did not understand," said Semi. "He came East as soon as his sentence was ended—though he has spent but small time inside prison walls the last few years—having made himself trusted there and been permitted exactly as he said to work on the State highways, where his ability was used. He came East to find you, my child, and he heard of Dorien's shooting and of you—"

"From whom?" the girl asked quickly.

"From Mr. Kornung, on whom he called. And having learned what Kornung told him, he did not endeavor to see you, but Dorien instead. He took a room and sought to reach him in an ordinary manner and was refused. But because his heart was inflamed against him, he was still determined to see him and avenge you as he tells me—unless he could compel him to do the honorable thing—"

"Compel him!" Roamer's daughter repeated. "Oh—my God! Wait—let me tell you now—how slight was his need—let me tell you what actually happened the night before the shooting—why it really happened—why Arch lost his head. I— Mr. Dual, you are right. I think Archer really loves me in the only way he knows. He—he has even offered to marry me, although marriage is a thing at which he scoffs—as he scoffs at everything good or pure or holy—as he even scoffs at God.

"He—he believes in nothing—but he would have married me, I think, really, had I consented. I—I think he wanted me more than anything in life. And—after he had brought Mr. Dorien and me together and saw how things were going—he could hardly fail to know the cause. I—I told him I wouldn't go through with it, and I knew he knew why by the look in his eyes. But he didn't say much at the time, and I hoped he understood. Then on the day before the shooting I got a letter. It was from a woman. I—I think now Archer must have got her to write. But then it drove me frantic.

"I—oh—I've got to speak frankly. You know Mr. Dorien's reputation—Mr. Dual has spoken of how he lived. And in this note this woman told me of their past associations. And then Archer Kell came to see me and told me the girl had told him she had written, and asked why I should have any mercy on a man like that. I"—she was panting now as she stood there—"it's hard to speak of these things, but I must—I must make you understand—how strangely everything happened. What that girl had written drove me frantic and I agreed with Archer that

I would do as he asked—and I suppose I would have kept my word but for one thing, if Mr. Dorien had acted differently.

"Anyway, I was to go to him that night and manage to remain with him till Archer appeared to pose as my brother. For though he had arranged the whole thing—planned it, that is—Mr. Dorien had never seen Archer, of course. But I took the letter with me, and because of what I felt I showed it to Mr. Dorien as soon as I was inside his rooms, and he read it, and—didn't deny it.

"He—he made a clean breast of it. He—he told me it was true and he was sorry—that he loved me—that he knew he wasn't worthy of me. And—and I—I couldn't stand it. I—I told him what I was—what I had been—what I had come there to accomplish—and I told him I was going away. And he said—he said: 'Does that mean that you love me?'

"And I—I couldn't lie to him and I told him 'Yes.' And then he laughed, and said that if that was so nothing else mattered and that now we each knew the worst of the other, I should stay where I was and when Kelley came, we would face him together. And that is what we did, though I was terribly afraid, and"—all at once a strange, little wistful smile formed itself upon her lips—"and glad. Mr Dorien called his Jap and had him sit where he could see us all night long, and we talked. I told him everything in my life worth telling—and it seemed to me the night would never pass.

"Then, just before ten, Kelley showed up as he had promised, and Mr. Dorien defied him, and told him he meant to marry me and Archer turned and asked me if that was right and I said it was. He didn't say anything more. He just drew an automatic and started shooting, and I screamed and ran over and seized his arm, and Kato ran in and broke it and took away his gun.

"After that we took Mr. Dorien to a hospital—Kato and I, that is, and he kept silent because he didn't want the notoriety the thing would bring upon me—and Archer knew that, but has kept threatening to kill him ever since—and sometimes I felt as if I were going crazy, and I went to Mr. Kornung and asked him to help me if he could. And then when you told me a man had been found on his fire escape, I was terribly frightened and I—I didn't know my own father!"

Her voice broke in hysterical laughter. "I—didn't know—my own father!"

"I guess possibly I've been a fool," Mrs. Meese spoke all at once. "But I was fooled myself. I didn't know when I was hired as her companion, what was going on. This man Kell told me she was a girl from the West with money, and I wasn't even suspicious for a time.

"And after that—well, I'd grown to be fond of her, and I knew she needed a woman more than anything else in the world—and if Mr. Dorien really married her in the end everything would be all right—so I kept staying on. And when she finally came over here yesterday and came home and told me she'd found a real friend, I went down on my knees to God."

"Matilda—why, Matilda!" Muriel turned to her.

And Mrs. Meese reached out and took her into her arms.

Johnson was fingering his chin. Bryce blew his nose with a sort of trumpet sound

"Does he know—about Jack and me?" Suddenly Muriel questioned. There was a slight flush in her face as she raised it from Mrs. Meese's breast

And Semi answered, smiling: "Aye, child—your father knows now and understands. Wherefore, his heart is no longer hardened against him, but exalted and lifted up because of the groundlessness of his fears."

Into my mind there leaned the mental picture of Julian Roamer's face as I had seen it that morning. And now I understood the strangeness of his manner—the ambiguity of his words—the almost exultant quality of his voice. They were those of a man exalted, lifted momentarily to a superlative plane of existence in the joy of a priceless possession found safe where he fancied it lost.

And as though he sensed my own comprehension of the matter, Semi went on speaking. "For there is more joy over the one lamb that was lost and is found than the ninety and nine in the fold."

"Can I go to him?" Muriel asked.

"Nay—child," Dual denied. "That, too, he understands, for I have told him that as yet the course of this matter is not run out—wherefore he is content to know you are with me, as I promised him you should be, till the wheel turns a little further, and passes, leaving the guilty ground into dust."

Once more there had crept into his words the odd, cryptic quality of expression in which he so often indulged—that quality which had caused Johnson to exclaim that he said two things at once.

But his meaning could scarcely be mistaken and it was Johnson who sought to make its meaning plainer.

"I reckon you mean Kelley?"

"Kelley," said Semi Dual, "shall soon be as though he had never been—his sun and his moon blotted out."

"But—" Johnson frowned. "If what you've said is correct, an' I reckon it is, why on earth did he try to shoot Roamer?"

"Did he?" Semi questioned.

"Huh?" Johnson stiffened "Oh, well—I get you. My man Lezner says it was him all right."

"And," said Semi Dual, "until my talk with Mr. Roamer I was unaware that Kelley was suspected. He told me he had overheard what Lezner said. It was then I conceived the thought of Miss Roamer's disappearance from the Kenton. We discussed it and agreed."

"Eh?" Johnson queried quickly. "I'm afraid I don't getchu."

"Have your men apprehended Kelley?" Dual suggested. "Suppose you ascertain before you answer."

He bent and withdrew a telephone standard and cord from a little cupboard sunk into one end of his desk.

Johnson complied.

"Not yet," he confessed as Dual relieved him of the instrument.

"Nor will they, in my estimation. The thing is not in his stars. But to answer your former question—he has dealt in the bodies of women for years—and for years there has been a woman whom he himself has desired. Wherefore, if beyond his present suspicions, that woman should seemingly disappear—"

It was almost Machiavellian in its conception and yet no more than a further illustration of how our strange friend worked, of the knowledge that enabled him to play on human emotions as a master plays on musical keys, with as certain and deft a touch. Kelley was wanted, and if he had really shot Roamer, he knew it and had taken cover in some secret haunt no doubt. But even so he would seek to communicate with Muriel Roamer—the child of the man he had wounded and at the same time the girl he had protected for himself, in a physical sense, at least.

All that dashed into my mind as Muriel Roamer cried out: "Is that why you asked me to stay here? Oh—Mr. Dual—I can't. It—it isn't certain that he knew it was my father last night any more than I did—and whatever he has done he has guarded me in a measure—always." She paused.

"As a man guards a thing he values," Semi Dual said slowly. "From a purely selfish motive, my child—to retain for himself— from no higher motive—degrading the spirit to his own sordid levels in so far as he was able—protecting merely the flesh. And should a man dig a pit for another and fall therein himself, who but himself may be blamed?"

"It's your notion to flush him into the open, by findin' her gone then?" Johnson resumed. "Well—I call that little short of clever—darned if I don't."

"Perhaps," said Semi slowly, "if cleverness lie in employing a man's known characteristics against him."

"But if it does flush him, why won't he be grabbed when he shows?" Plainly Johnson was puzzled.

"One seeks for a man or an answer where it lies, in order to find it," Semi Dual returned.

The inspector frowned. "D'ye mean you know where he is yourself?"

"No, Mr. Johnson—certainly not at this time."

"Then—"

"Peace—patience yet a little while the Wheel of Justice turns. What is written, is written and the hour of that one's doom approaches, in what manner I myself know not—save that it is the end."

"You don't know?" Johnson gaped.

"No. I read only what his sign portends."

"Well—all right," Johnson yielded. "Then I reckon we simply mark time?"

"Mark time, yes." said Semi. "Time which marks, and measures and adjusts all things."

"But—Jack—Mr. Dorien," Muriel Roamer spoke again. "What will he think when he finds I'm not at the Kenton?"

Semi smiled as he answered. "Let not such considerations disturb you. For I shall ask my friend Glace, and Mr. Bryce, if he so elects, to wait upon him now in a little while, and explain to him that here in my garden you are about to find the answer to all questions of the heart. Peace—child. I shall speak with you later—at more length. And you, Gordon"—he turned to me directly—"may I ask you to see to this latest mission?"

"At once," I agreed and took up my hat.

Jim and Johnson went with me, out across the noontide quiet of the roof.

CHAPTER XVII

"THE WHEEL IS TURNING"

"THERE'S SOMETHIN' HE ain't sayin'," Bryce began once we were back in our office and I had rung up Dorien, asked if he had called the Kenton that morning, and told him we were coming over to explain when he snapped back a quick inquiry as to what I was talking about.

"There's always somethin' he ain't ready to say when he talks like that. But—anyway, Kelley seems due to get his."

Johnson eyed him. "Did you ever try puttin' two an' two together?" he suggested. "You ought to—once. He was giving me a tip to cover Monks Hall pretty close, I guess, when he asked you two to go over an' wise up Dorien as to this disappearance stunt.

"Wake up, Jim—when Kelley finds she's dropped out of sight along with Mrs. Meese, what's he goin' to think? What's any man as jealous as he is of another goin' to think right off? Dorien, eh? He'll dope it Dorien's got her out of the way, an' he'll try to get at him, an'—if he gets hurt resistin' arrest, that ain't my fault. I don't particularly care whether he does or not. He's a bad actor an' he won't be missed such an awful lot. Well, there you are I admit I never got hep to Roamer—but I doubt if Kelley did, either, th' way this is workin' out. I didn't even know she had a livin' father from th' start. Otherwise I had it pretty near right."

"Then," I said, "your idea is we should warn Dorien concerning Kelley?"

"Warn him?" Johnson chuckled. "Well, yes—though I don't guess that bird will pay much attention. He ain't th' sort to hole up if he knows th' girl is safe."

"See here"—Jim reentered the conversation—"if Kelley didn't know Roamer, why—did he shoot him?"

Johnson retorted with a counterquestion. "Why did he if he did—why shoot his girl's father? That looks to me like a darned poor move."

"An' why did Kornung have Roamer at his house—if he was an ex-convict—instead of an engineer, like he said?"

Johnson chuckled. "You're gettin' worse all th' time, old boy. Kornung raised th' girl like she told us. Probably Roamer told him about his play for Dorien, an' Kornung told him to come over there and behave, till they could straighten things out in a little bit safer way. He knew him, of course."

"Then why was Kelley hidin' in th' garage?"

"My Gawd!" Johnson said, "you're worse than a kid. Go ask Dual an' see if he'll tell you. I don't know myself. Now I'm goin' down an' put some men on Monks Hall, an' you 'tend to your job."

"Yes," I agreed, "come along. We don't know the answer yet. Let Kelley hang himself."

Frankly, though, I was as puzzled by Jim's final question as were my companions, and the thing kept nagging away in my brain all the way over to Park Drive. Why had Kelley seem-ingly trailed the father of the girl he plainly meant to hold to himself and shot him down in Kornung's garage? It seemed an utterly senseless action unless—unless Kelley had been afraid of Roamer himself—had feared him as the parent of the girl he had led into evil ways through the last few years. Self-pres-ervation! Was that it? The first law of Nature! As Johnson confessed I didn't know and yet some way I felt Dual did, if he chose to speak in anything save his cryptic symbols of speech.

We found Dorien waiting us in an evident impatience.

"What's this about my calling the Kenton?" he burst out as

soon as we were inside his quarters. "As a matter of fact, I did, but they told me that both Miss Roamer and Mrs. Meese, her companion, were out."

"They told you the truth," I informed him. "It is about that we want to speak."

I went on and put him briefly in touch with the facts. At the end he was looking a trifle dazed.

"Roamer? It was Roamer who was shot at Korning's place last night—her father—the man they caught m my fire escape? Well I'm damned!" he said.

"Julian Roamer," I agreed.

He nodded. "She told me all about her father, Mr. Glace, but—good Lord—he was after a showdown with me?"

"Exactly."

He grinned. "He'd have had an easy time persuading me if he'd got in, I guess. Is he badly wounded?"

"Not at all," I assured him. "And he understands the whole situation now."

"Thanks to this friend of yours who has taken her to this odd place where he hangs out. Gad! I never dreamed there was anything out of the usual run on the Urania roof. You say he worked this whole thing out from studying her birth date and mine and that of Kelley and her father—really?"

"Precisely. And—she wanted you to understand. That's why he asked us to come over here. Incidentally, Kelley may start something when he finds she isn't at the Kenton."

"And thinks I'm back of it?" he said quickly and laughed. "This friend of yours says he's about due to cash in?"

"Yes."

"Well," he went on, smiling. "I wouldn't mind helping him verify the prediction if friend Kelley wants to take a chance."

"This building is watched," I told him. "He'll meet a warm reception if he does."

"Oh, piffle!" Dorien shrugged. "That's your man Johnson, I

suppose. He's certainly on the job. I don't need police protection. But—I'd like to meet this man Semi Dual. He must be an unusual sort, and I owe him something—for what he's done for—Muriel—for both of us—I guess. Anyway, I can meet him and tell him so, Mr. Glace."

"I fancy there will be opportunity before this is over," I said, since it seemed probable to me that Dual would come into contact with the man in person before he withdrew from his affairs.

"Over?" he repeated. "Why—it's pretty well over now so far as she and I and her father are concerned, isn't it, Mr. Glace? Or—do you mean Kelley? Let the man go, can't you? I don't care whether he's apprehended or not. If he gets away it would quite possibly be the easiest all around, I should judge."

"Kelley won't get away, Mr. Dorien," I declared out of my faith in Semi, and the correctness of such predictions as he permitted himself to make. I'd seen too many of them work out in the past.

"Eh? You believe all this friend of yours says?" He eyed me. "I'll admit he's been infernally clever, but—how can he tell a man's going to die?"

Bryce cut in. "Th' same way he knew you an' Muriel Roamer would fall in love if you ever came together. That's right, Dorien, an' when I used to be on the force I was a fairly hard-headed cop. This man ain't guessin—he knows."

"But good Lord!" Dorien got up and moved about. Presently he halted in front of Jim. "I've heard of such things, gentlemen, but this man really does them?"

"Yep," Bryce nodded. "He does 'em. He's got it down to a science, Mr. Dorien."

The man breathed deeply. "He said—Muriel and I would love if we ever met. He says Kelley's race is nearly run. Gentlemen, did you ever hear a poem entitled 'Fate'?"

I looked at Jim and intercepted his glance directed in my direction.

"Dual was quotin' it about this business the other day," he returned.

" 'Two shall be born?'" Dorien frowned slightly. "I used to laugh at such things, but—I'm not laughing now. The whole thing's strange. Look here, can her father see visitors, do you suppose?"

"I see no reason why not," I replied. "He was sitting up on a back rest this morning, and appeared in an exceedingly cheerful mood."

"Then by jove—I'm going over and see him. D'ye think I might?"

"Why not?" I made answer. "I think quite probably he would be glad to have you come to him, man to man. I can imagine that in his position I would appreciate such an action,"

"Unless Kelley catches you," said Bryce.

Dorien laughed. "Kelley isn't catching any one, Mr. Bryce. He's doubtless in hiding since your man Dual takes such a dramatic means of trying to bring him out. I'll do it. I'll go over there this afternoon and we'll have a talk, get acquainted. Lord—everything's coming out all right. Gentlemen, I can't tell you how much I appreciate your interest and efforts in all this, even if I did balk when you came to see me first."

"An' offer to have Kato demonstrate his arm breakin' ability on us," Jim grinned.

Dorien's eyes twinkled. "Kato is a valuable man, and close mouthed, but"—he sobered—"it was really the little girl who saved my life."

"You've got to thank Johnson, too, for smoothing out the wrinkles," I remarked as I rose. "He dragged Bryce and me into your affairs, and through us, Semi Dual."

He nodded. "I quite appreciate that, Mr. Glace. I seem to have a great many people to thank—and I do really. I feel a trifle overwhelmed, to tell the truth."

We shook hands and left him and went back to the office.

And once there, just by ourselves, Jim drew a deep and audible breath.

"And now what? What is it Semi expects to happen?" he asked. "What's this thing about a long deferred justice? Do you make it, son? Does he mean Kelley?"

"I don't know what he means, Jim," I confessed, just as Miss Nellie Newell tapped on the door and slipped inside.

"Mr. Glace, your friend Mr. Dual sent for Danny after you left, and Dan came back about an hour later and went right out again without leaving any word except to tell you he was on an assignment."

"Very well, Nellie," I said and waited until she had withdrawn, and looked into my partner's face.

"Dual sent him—somewhere," I said with a strange full feeling in my throat.

"Just like he did at first," he chimed in, his eyes beginning to fire with an avidly speculative light.

"On an assignment," I repeated Miss Newell's repetition of Danny's message.

"He knows, son." Bryce reached for the telephone standard. "I tell you he knows."

"What are you going to do?" I questioned.

"Call Johnson." He put the number through.

I sat and waited and presently he spoke—waited—spoke again, obviously to the inspector this time, since he rapidly told him of Semi's action.

And then he listened.

"He did?" he said at length. "Well—all right. Oh, sure, I get it. Kornung knew the girl."

He swung about after setting the instrument down with a bang. "Dual called him an hour ago and told him not to fail to cover Kornung's house."

But—I had gathered the fact beforehand from his words. "Kornung's?" I said. "On the chance Kelley goes back there?"

Jim nodded. "Sure, son—it's the other end of the bet. Dorien loved her an' Kelley knew it—knows Kornung knows her—knows she was goin' to see him. Remember what Dan heard over that telephone arrangement? Dorien and Kornung's th' first two he's goin' to think of when he finds she ain't at th' hotel. See it?"

"Oh, pip! Of course you see it. So does Johnson. You got to hand it to Semi for never sleepin' on a bet. An' Johnson ain't sleepin' either. He's been down to th' hotel an' had a chin with th' day operator on th' switchboard. She says somebody's called th' girl's suite a dozen times to-day an' it was always th' same voice—an' a man's voice at that.

"Get it? It's plain enough, ain't it? That guy's goin' to wait just about so long, an' then wake up to th' fact that he's gypped. An' then he's goin' to be in to make medicine, an' it 'll be bad. Semi's wrote his ticket just about right. After he's worked himself up just about so far he's goin' on th' warpath, an' that's where he gets his."

As it chanced, he wasn't so far wrong, either, though the thing happened somewhat differently from what any of us, except Dual in his own inscrutable estimation of all the human values, would have been likely to predict. He alone of us all, I can truthfully say in the light of what is now but one more past demonstration of that law of immutable justice in which he believed, had any full or complete conception of where or how the sword of that justice was to strike. And as I have already made sufficiently plain, he did not see fit to speak.

Still that was all no more than foreshadowed then, as Jim and I continued our supposititious discussion until at length Bryce rose and went over to his own room. I called Nellie in and we ran over some correspondence. At its end I questioned her concerning Dan's departure. But she had nothing to add, and she laughed.

"That kid! 'Tell Mr. Glace I'm on an assignment.' They were his exact words, Mr. Glace, and he looked as important as if he'd been told to go out and turn the crank that moves the world."

I nodded. I could imagine Danny's sense of a vast responsibility resting upon his youthful shoulders—too, his interest in serving the interests of Muriel Roamer—the girl who had impulsively planted a kiss on his freckled face and thereby earned the loyalty of his stanch little heart. And from that my thoughts leaped to Dorien calling upon her father—and the girl waiting in Semi's garden—and the rose she had held that morning in her fingers, when we had come upon her there at his side.

"That's all, Nellie," I said.

She left me and I went on with my reveries. I can scarcely call them anything else. Wheels within wheels, Dual had said and it seemed a good description of the thing from first to last. Wheels within wheels.

Into my musing the little telephone on the wall cut sharply with its buzz.

I stiffened to attention, rose and answered.

"Gordon," came the voice of Semi Dual, "see to it that either yourself or Bryce is continuously in the office throughout to-morrow. You saw Dorien?"

"Yes," I said. "He understands. But—Semi—"

"Peace." He checked my plea for some definite indication almost before I began it. "To-morrow's light should show the sentence of a man's own deeds descend upon him. The wheel is turning and—it grinds exceedingly fine, my friend."

CHAPTER XVIII

DANNY QUINN'S TIP

THE WORDS OF Semi Dual rang in my head the rest of that afternoon. To me they meant but one thing, and that thing death—the death of the man Archer Kell, when pronounced by the lips of the man who had already announced his impending doom.

I told Bryce, and he called Johnson again and told him, and Johnson fumed a bit, because no trace of Kelley had been found. The dragnet was still spread and at no place had the man it was spread to gather come into contact with any of its human strands.

To-morrow, then, I thought—but as to what to-morrow was actually to bring, I never dreamed.

It came. Jim and I clung leechlike to what had come to be our station—a sort of listening post, where we should come in contact with the first intimation of events. The morning hours dragged. So literal was our application of Dual's direction that we had lunch sent in. One o'clock came and two and three. Bryre smoked innumerable cigars. Four o'clock, and still nothing—not even a sign of Dan, who had left on his assignment the previous afternoon.

Four fifteen—and the whirr of the telephone on my desk. I reached for it—dragged it to me, answered the ring.

"Mr. Glace!" The voice of Danny Quinn. I felt my heart stagger in its beating.

"Dan!" I exclaimed.

151

"Listen." His accents were lowered.

"Kelley just come down here to the Stroller Building where Kornung has his offices an' went in. Mr. Dual told me to tell you if he did, an' for you to tell Johnson, an' get down here on th' jump! I'll be waitin'.'"

His receiver snapped up.

"Kelley!" My heart started racing with a heavy force. Kelley at Kornung's office probably—almost certainly Kelley! Tell Johnson but what was the use? The wheel had been turning all day and for days and years—still—

"Kelley's just gone up to Kornung's office in the Stroller Building," I snapped at Bryce and called the Central Station not quite as calmly as I might had my emotions been less intense.

Johnson was waiting. He had said he would be. I told him what Dan had said.

"Gawd!" I heard him mouth, and then: "All right. Get over. I'll be with you."

I reached for my hat. Bryce was ready. We ran out and waited with what patience we could for an elevator cage.

The Stroller Building was not more than a five minute walk, at the pace we made. It loomed tall, massive, immobile, with no hint of any impending climax in human affairs as we approached. How long, I wondered, had it taken Dan to reach a telephone after he had seen his man—the man I now knew he had been placed to watch for—go inside its doors.

"Got your gun?" Beside me Bryce was breathing hoarsely.

I nodded.

"Then—well go right up."

I nodded again. We would go right up—and see how fine the wheel had ground. Kelley and Kornung—this was the end.

We reached the Stroller entrance.

And there was Dan, his face avid with tense waiting, his lips speaking swiftly.

"He ain't come back. Kornung's up there—912. Where's Johnson?"

"Coming," I said. "Wait here and tell him we've gone up."

A car was filling. We crowded in it and it started. One—two—three floor, and a stop; five—six, and another. A down car passed swiftly. Seven—eight—

"Nine!" I called.

It stopped again, and the door was slid back. We hurried out. Nine hundred before us—nine hundred one, two, three to the right. A door flew open and a young man ran out. He turned toward us, hesitated, paused. His eyes were staring, wide. The door behind him was numbered 912.

Something had happened. I knew it.

"Belong in there?" I asked.

"Ye-es. Are you—police?" he faltered.

I nodded. It wasn't literally true, but close enough.

"Somebody's shot!" he gasped, and turned beside us as we ran inside and across an outer office where two or three girl stenographers stood in a huddled, pallid-faced group, toward a farther door.

It was locked!

I turned my eyes to the youth.

"I—tried it," he said, "just before I telephoned the station. There was a man went in there fifteen minutes ago about— and not more than five minutes ago there was a shot!"

"Come on!" I prompted Jim, and set my shoulder to the barrier before us. It resisted. Bryce drew back and hurled his additional weight against it. The lock tore out of the jamb with a splintering of wood. We stumbled into a farther room and paused. It was a private office, sumptuously appointed, and at first it seemed empty, undisturbed. That, though, was at the first glance only. A step carried us toward a heavy, flat-topped desk, and beyond it the body of a man lay stretched face downward on the heavy pile of a handsome rug.

Kelley—I had never seen the man to know him, but I knew him then past any doubt. Kelley—his figure was clean limbed—his clothing almost dapper, Kelley—not Kornung, whom I had seen in his own house. Kelley, shot down and lying there before me. The wheel had turned and ground him into the dust.

I went toward him, put a hand upon him, turned him over. He moaned slightly as I did so and opened his eyes.

"Here," I said to the youth who had followed, "take that cushion out of that chair and put it under his head."

He complied in silence.

"Kelley?" I said.

"Yes"—a husky whisper.

"What happened?"

No answer—but a froth of blood on his lips.

"Kelley?"

His eyes were on mine. His lips moved. "Water!"

The pale-faced youth brought it in a glass.

Kelley drank as I held up his head.

"He got me," he said, his voice a trifle stronger.

I nodded. "Kornung?" I questioned.

Heavy footsteps sounded, and Johnson thrust his way into the room and came swiftly to us, went down upon a knee.

"Kelley!" he said. "Kornung shot him? Your boy says he came down just as you came up—stuck a gun into the elevator boy's ribs an' made him drop straight through, ran out and made off." His eyes jerked to the pale-faced youth. "What do you know about it? Did he come out through the office before he left?"

"No, sir," the youth declared. "I guess he must have gone out that door over there." He pointed to what was plainly a second means of egress from the room.

The wounded man turned his eyes to the city detective. "Hello, Johnson," he said. "Kornung got me. Send somebody over to his house to get him—and—get that girl. He's double-crossed me—but—I'm going to get him just the same."

"Wait!" Johnson sprang up and seized a telephone on the desk. He called the station and spoke swiftly, hung up, and returned.

"That's all right," he announced, as much to Jim and me as to Kelley. "They will go over there and get in touch with a couple of men I've got watching his house already. They'll let him go in, but—he won't get out again."

"You got men over—there?" Kelley questioned.

Johnson nodded.

"That's good. Johnson—I'm done in. Kornung shot me. You know the girl, Roma Temple. It was over her. He's got her somewhere. I came up here—to ask him—I wanted her. Johnson—wanted her—for years—damn this blood in my—lungs. Water!"

I held the glass to the lips of the speaker, and he drank again. "Thanks. Listen, Johnson—I'm dying—I guess. And it's a sort of deathbed confession. It won't help me, but it will get Kornung an' put that girl in th' clear when you get her. Be sure to get her, Johnson—an' ask about her old man—Julian Roamer—Roamer's her right name—Muriel Roamer."

"Yes—I know that." Johnson prompted. "Go on. Anything you say now will stand at law."

"I know it," Kelley said. "I—I've got to go back fifteen years—a long time, Johnson. I was just a kid. I was on a job—reclamation project out West. Kornung was chief engineer—Roamer was with him. The paymaster was held up one night—killed. Andrew Kornung and I did it. We didn't mean to kill him, but he put up a fight.

"Kornung had been speculating—had to have money. He dragged me into it. He's a cold-blooded devil. After he killed the man—he told me under the law of that State I was as deep in it as he was. We got the money and ran back to his shack and hid the cash, under the mattress of his bunk. We agreed to swear we'd both been sitting there when the killing happened—alibi, you know, and all that stuff.

"We got in without anybody seeing, and sat there and talked it all over. Muriel's father came along and found the body. He was bending over it when some others of the men on the work came up. He was arrested and tried. They gave him an indeterminate sentence, because they couldn't find any sign of the gun the man was killed with—or the swag—element of doubt, you know. God I can't breathe!"

I lifted him in my arms and let him lean back against my shoulder, and after a time he sighed. "That's better. They convicted Roamer—he was a widower with one child Muriel. Kornung took her—told Roamer he'd take care of—educate her and all that. Well—he did. He and I left there soon after and came East. The man's a crook—a sort of Jekyll-Hyde. He's a crook because he's crooked by nature. This engineering stuff was all a pose. He started me crooked with that deal out West and he's kept me crooked ever since, but neither one of us could squeal on the other without turning in himself. He—he organized a gang to bleed rich men—through women—oh I guess you know, all right."

Johnson nodded. "Yep—I've been hep for some time, but I thought you was th' head of that bunch."

"I was," the dying man assented, "in name. Kornung was the brains an' th' scout all the time. He went into society—he picked the fall guys nearly every time. He planned to use Muriel after she had finished school, after she was educated as a lady qualified to play the part—and when she was ready, he told me to trap her into a compromising situation and then whip her into the game

"I—I did it but I've looked out for her—seen she didn't come to any harm. I—on the level, Johnson—she meant more to me than any other thing. That's how we've gone on. Then after I shot Dorien—oh, yes, I shot him because I knew he'd come to love her, and she him—and he said they meant to marry—why—her father shows up all at once.

"The board—had terminated his sentence, and he hit it East

first thing. He saw Kornung—and Kornung told him his girl had gone to the bad: that he'd ordered her out of his home—played the damned hypocrite—and told me what he'd done. Then Roamer went after Dorien, and you nabbed him, and he came and told Kornung after you'd flushed him, and after he'd spied and seen Muriel come to his house. Kornung told him to come over and put up with him. And he told me we'd got to get him out of the way, because he knew too much—he'd told Kornung he meant to spend the rest of his life finding the man who had murdered Pete Skovill—that was the paymaster's name. So—give me another drink.

"So," he went on after he had moistened his mouth. "Kornung rigged up that garage stunt, and he was to shoot Roamer while he pretended to shoot me. I—I balked at killing Muriel's father, and he agreed to do the trick. I fell into his trap. I know now he meant to get me, too, and get rid of both Roamer and me, and make it look like he'd killed in self-defense. But I didn't see it then, and I hid as we'd agreed, and the first shot he fired went right through my coat, and then I woke up.

"Roamer dropped and then I heard one of your men, as it turned out, yelling, and Kornung spoke to me. 'Beat it,' he said, and I ran, and threw my gun into the bull's face. But Roamer wasn't dead, and Kornung couldn't finish the job, as you know—and he tried another trick. He took Muriel away from the Kenton, or I think he did. I was lying holed up because Kornung told me your man had recognized me. But after I couldn't get her, I doped it out—that he'd got her somewhere, and was goin' to use her against Roamer—to stop his mouth, you know—in case he got wise—because Roamer wasn't unconscious—and Kornung was afraid he'd overheard him tell me to get out when your man ran up, and might work things out.

"I—didn't run far, you know—just into the basement of his house at first—and after they'd took Roamer away we had a talk—and I left. He was pretty well worked up, and I decided he'd made up his mind to save himself. So to-day I came down here and asked him—where—Muriel—was. And—he wouldn't tell me—and I—reached for my—gun—but he—beat me to it. And—that's all. Go get him—make him—pay. And—find—her—take her to—her father—tell him—she's a—good girl—tell him—I kept her that—way. Tell—her—"

The froth on his lips grew darker—grew quite dark. He choked.

"Look out!" said Johnson tensely. "That's the end of him. Kornung—Gawd!"

He stood up as I lowered the dead man's head to the leather cushion from the chair of the man who had been his evil genius for years.

"Come along," he went on. "Let's get over there and finish the job. Don't touch a thing you—" to the pale-faced youth. "Stay here—all of you—till I send a man up to take charge."

He strode heavily back through the outer office and hurried toward the bank of elevators.

Jim and I followed at his heels. "Tell—her—" Kelley's never ended message to the little opposing Venus kept ringing in my ears. "Tell her—tell her—" What should I tell her, I wondered, and decided that I would tell her he had tried to say he loved her—had thought of her in the moment when he died. Life was strange, full of strange angles, wheels within wheels. Suddenly there leaped into my brain Dual's cryptic mention of a justice long deferred, and I thought I comprehended: justice not on Kelley, but on Kornung—the arch rogue.

The elevator reached the bottom, and we left it. There was Danny.

"Go back to the office," I told him quickly. "It's all over. Kelley's dead."

Then I hastened after Johnson, who was climbing into a police machine at the curb.

"Stop at the first peg post on th' way an' then get over to 1022 Harrison Avenue," he directed, as I clambered in with Bryce.

Johnson told the officer on post to telephone for men to take charge at Kornung's office, and roared on again, regardless of traffic regulations, with the certain privilege in their overriding of those by whom they are enforced.

Kornung—had he really gone to his house? Kelley had said so, but—would he have done so? Perhaps. He might even have deemed it essential, before seeking to escape, in order to get papers—money—things that might be needful to his further course.

Kornung—who had sent Muriel Roamer's father to prison for his own crime through fifteen vanished years—Kornung, who had betrayed Roamer's trust—betrayed his promise to care for his child.

We roared to a skidding stand before his house. A car stood close to the curb before us.

Johnson uttered an exclamation.

"He's here! That's his!"

We sprang up. A man came sauntering along the street. He paused and spoke to the inspector.

"He drove up here a little while ago, and went in like he was in a hurry."

Johnson nodded. "All right, Lezner—keep a watch out. Come on, boys."

He forged ahead, straight for the front doors. Without hesitation he placed his hand on the knob. It yielded and he pushed the door before him. We pressed in closely together.

Johnson produced a service automatic. A stairway curved upward before us. There were doors to right and left. For an instant we stood in a silence broken only by the whisper of our breathing, and then from the head of the stairs the voice of an unseen speaker descended:

"That's far enough, inspector. Stop!"

CHAPTER XIX

JUSTICE LONG DEFERRED

"KORNUNG!" I WANT to put it down here that Johnson showed the cold courage of his nature. He kept cool. In a position where he certainly knew that he was a plain target for a known murderer—a man who inside the past hour had shed a fellow being's blood—he never altered, never gave back.

"Well?" came the voice of the unseen speaker.

"The jig's up You killed Kelley—but he didn't die till he'd spilled the facts on that Skovill murder Roamer's been doin' time for—"

For the third time Kornung spoke, interrupting: "Which should show you that I have no high regard for human life."

Most amazingly as I stood there I realized that in this exceedingly tense moment, where heart beats might spell the space of life remaining to any one of us four, the man, like Johnson, was seemingly cool, able to perceive and make a point, which in its very making was palpably a threat.

Johnson seemed to weigh the words before he answered.

"Well, admittin' that, it boils down to this: do you want to take it quiet or—shoot it out?"

"I'm a straight shot, Johnson!"

"But you didn't kill Roamer night before last."

"Well, no—" slowly, as though the man were digesting this further proof of knowledge on the part of the police; and then: "I presume the house is surrounded?"

"You're a good guesser."

"You work quickly, inspector."

"Had you watched for days."

A pause, and then: "Really? I confess you surprise me. Then your man Lezner was merely on the job the other night."

"He was."

"Then—I can't escape?"

"Not a chance. Oh, you may get me or one of these boys, but—what's the use? Come along quiet, Kornung."

"No, thanks. You see, I know what it means, inspector."

I located the voice. The man was standing just inside a door near the head of the stairs, from where he could command our every move. I whispered the information to Johnson.

His grip tightened on the weapon in his grasp. His lips rolled back slightly, showing the white line of his teeth.

"Then—" His voice came gruffly.

"This!" The word was followed by a shot.

I am convinced now that Kornung did not try to do any execution; that he fired merely to cover his move, to hold us there for a heart beat. But the bullet plunged into the wall back of Johnson and spattered plaster in a tiny shower over the three of us.

Johnson uttered a sort of inarticulate bellow and let off his own weapon twice, just as the door from inside which Kornung had fired was slammed shut and the bolt shot to in its latch.

The next moment we were charging up the stairs, each now with his weapon in his hand.

We reached the stairhead, and Johnson voiced a caution.

"Steady!"

He edged toward the door along the wall, put out a hand, and tried the knob. It did not yield.

He glanced at Jim and me. Determination was in his eyes.

"Get him if he gets me," was all he said as he drew back and hurled all his weight against the door.

Oh, yes—he was brave, because he knew very well what

chance he might be taking—the sort of a man who had locked it in his face. He had just come from a bit of his gruesome handiwork. But he did not hesitate.

He flung himself at the door and it yielded. The three of us plunged through it. We stood in what I judged was Kornung's bedroom, from its fittings—and the open door of a little wall safe to one side.

"Get back there!" The words came in at an open window through which, for a single instant, it had flashed on me Kornung had leaped.

There was a farther door, leading possibly to a bath. It was closed. I glanced toward it. Somewhere another door crashed.

Johnson charged. Again the door gave before him. I saw enough to tell me there was a bathroom beyond it, and then I turned and ran out into the upper hall, just as Kornung emerged from the door of a room a little way along it, as I had fancied he might. It was an old house—and they are sometimes found with a bath between two bedrooms.

"Johnson—Bryce!" I yelled, as he fired.

No doubt but he meant to stop me then. His bullet fanned my cheek, I returned the shot, but my hand, I confess, was unsteady. He dived for a rear stairs, and I ran down the front with Johnson and Jim, by now at my heels.

At the bottom I turned down the lower hall to the rear, but Kornung had too much start. He ran straight into the kitchen and—there was a man outside its door—on a small rear porch.

Kornung fired twice—and the man outside—Lezner—once. A woman—Kornung's cook—started screaming.

He spun about and came straight back at us shooting. But by now exertion had made his aim too unsteady. Suddenly he wrenched open a door on his right and plunged through it out of sight. Beyond it his feet clattered on a flight of stairs.

"Down!" Johnson bellowed. "Lezner, watch the cellar windows. He's a trapped rat now, all right." He drew a heavy hand across his forehead. "Either of you boys hurt?"

"Come on," Bryce urged and laid a hand on the latch of the door through which Kornung had vanished. His lids were narrowed to slits, his blood suffusing his face, and he was breathing harshly.

"Wait," Johnson stayed him. "He's got one shot left. I counted. He shot Kelley and he's fired eight times. Did you see that bag in his hand? That's what he come over here for. Reckon you spotted that open safe."

I nodded.

"Well," Jim urged, "for a man what brags about his shootin', I ain't seen nothin' yet. Come on; I'll take a chance."

Johnson frowned. "All right," he agreed. "Glace, you stay here, if he gets by us an' makes a break for th' top. You're married. Now, then, Jim, go ahead."

Bryce wrenched the door open on the word. He stepped through it, and Johnson followed. They went slowly down the stairs. Plainly they led to the cellar. I recalled that Kelley had said he hid there the night of Roamer's shooting, as they disappeared. And now Kornung was driven down there, cornered, at bay, like a rat, as Johnson said.

Silence then for a moment, save for the footfalls of the two men in the gloom down the throat of the stairs—the sound of a stumble, and a grunting, involuntary exclamation from Bryce.

Then the voice of Johnson: "Kornung—we've got you. Lay down and call it a day."

The words came back up the shaft of the stairway plainly to my ears. I edged down one step, two, peering into the shadows where my companions moved.

"Kornung—come out of it. Th' game's up."

My fingers, groping to steady me as I stood craning forward, encountered a button on the side of the staircase wall. I spoke, calling softly; "Johnson—shall I turn on the light down there?"

His answer came quickly. "Wait a minute. Bryce—get over to the other side. He's got only one shot left. All right up there, old man—turn 'er on."

"Wait!" As my fingers tightened on the button—one of the old time sort you turned instead of punched—Kornung spoke.

"Johnson, you're right—the game's up. But it's been a good game for years. I've fooled you, Johnson. I've fooled the whole kit and kaboodle of you. You'd never have got wise if it hadn't been for Roamer—in a million years. Oh, you dicks! Think you've got me, don't you? Think you're going to send me to the chair? Well, listen—listen closely—there's always one road out."

"Lights!" Johnson's voice rose in a bellow. "Kornung!"

There came a single muffled shot.

I turned the button and ran down the stairs.

And there, with Johnson and Bryce, I found Hubert Kornung, huddled down, back of a bin, part full of withering potatoes— dead by his own hand—like a cornered rat, indeed. And here, I thought, as I stood looking down upon him, while Johnson drew out the body and ordered its limbs in a gloomy silence, was what Semi Dual had meant when he spoke of a justice long deferred.

Johnson straightened. "And that ends it. Let him lay till we can send an' get him," he said. Just that—casual, matter of fact, as though it was all in the day's work, now that the man we had finally run to earth was no more than a chilling bit of clay.

We went back up the stairs and found a man, badly shaken, the remaining member of Kornung's household staff. But he knew little.

Johnson opened the bag Kornung had carried with him to the last. It was filled with a mass of currency and papers, dumped in hurriedly from the safe in his bedroom.

He snapped it shut. "All right, boys. I'll stay here and see what I can find, and use the phone a bit. Go out and tell Jerry to drive you over to your place if you want to, and come back. Tell Dual I'll see him after I get things straightened out."

We took him at his word. Jim lighted a cigar, and the police machine ran us over. It put us down in front of the Urania entrance, and we made our way to the roof.

It lay there under the rays of the late June day—slanting across it in a golden light—calm, peaceful, quiet, yet filled as we reached it with life.

Muriel Roamer and Dorien—and Roamer—the latter with his wounded shoulder eased by a sling beneath his elbow, seated beside the little fountain where the lily pads were floating. Semi Dual in his white and purple robes, and Mrs. Meese.

Their eyes turned to us as we appeared, and Semi spoke:

"It is finished!"

"Finished," I assented. "Kelley and Kornung are dead. Kornung shot Kelley, and later—himself."

Muriel cried out—a wordless little sound—and stood up, wide-eyed, lips parted against the golden light.

"Peace," said Semi Dual. "Tell me."

I complied. And at the end I told how Kelley in dying had sought to send a farewell message to the girl he had wanted, and, wanting, had managed to guard from major harm through all the sordid years.

She was weeping when I finished.

"Even yet I can hardly believe it," she declared. "I never dreamed Mr. Kornung had a part in Archer's work."

Roamer nodded. "Neither did I till the other night. Then I heard him tell the man to make his get-away, just before Lezner showed up. And I told Mr. Dual here about it at the hospital yesterday morning—by then I'd just about figured it out."

"And yesterday, after she came here to remain with me briefly," said Semi Dual, "Miss Roamer told me the date of Kornung's birth. The rest was easy. Once having erected his figure, everything checked out. No man lives to himself alone, and his figure fitted into the scheme of the entire matter, as shown by the others already at my disposal. The conclusion was past any doubt. He was saturnine in every characteristic—he died like a child of Saturn, in darkness, by his own hand, driven down into the earth. So in the end is the measure of a man's sin returned upon him, to crush him into nothingness. For it is written that as one soweth so shall one inevitably reap, and he who sows the wind shall reap the whirlwind, and he who sows good deeds shall reap—peace."

The words fell softly, tuned well-nigh, as it seemed, to the tinkle of the little fountain beside which he sat. And then his strong face lighted. He turned to Dorien and the girl, still standing.

"And for you, my children—this: The past and the future are the present—for no man has to himself more than the beating of a heart to employ. Wherein the past makes the present, and the future comes not, since it is but the present when it arrives. And this is fate—that some day out of darkness *two* shall meet, and read life's meaning in each other's eyes. Live in the present— forget the past. The future, so long as ye live the present rightly, lies with yourselves."

"But, you—you," said Muriel Roamer, and choked. "What— can I say to you, who have given me this present to live?" Her voice was shaken and at the last it broke.

"This," said Semi, smiling. "That a field, though barren, when scored by the plowshare of past suffering and crossed by the hand of the sower, and watered by earnest tears, shall yet bear much good fruit. Daughter—the key of all happiness lies in the wish to—serve. Those who bring sunshine into the lives of others cannot keep it out of their own."

"Which reminds me," Roamer remarked, "that, now every- thing is settled, I can go back West. Before I came East, I saw the man who was Governor when I was tried, and we had a rather lengthy talk. I convinced him I didn't kill Skovill, and he has a good deal of influence out there yet. He told me that after I got in touch with Muriel—he'd use it to get me a job." His eyes lighted with a quiet twinkle. "In fact, he said if I'd come back there, he'd put me to work—for the State."

"Dad!" Muriel turned to him. There were tears in her eyes— but a soft smile on her lips.

ABOUT THE AUTHOR:
DR. J.U. GIESY

BORN NEAR CHILLICOTHE, Ohio, August 6, 1877. That makes me a Buckeye, and some people have suggested that I was a nut. Of my actual birth I have no recollection. So this is mere hearsay evidence. When I was eight months of age my parents removed to southeastern Kansas and took me with them, as I was still unable to shift for myself.

When I was thirteen we again removed to Utah, where I received my common school education in common with other youngsters of a similar age. In 1895, I entered the Starling Medical College, Columbus, Ohio, and received my medical degree from that institution in 1898.

Returning to Salt Lake, I served an internship in a local hospital and have practiced medicine in that city ever since, with the exception of the time I spent in the United States service during the World War as a captain in the Medical Corps. As regards the Army I am still a major in the Reserve, attached to the Division Surgeon's Office of the 104th Division. In 1916 I was instrumental in organizing the first Plattsburg camp ever held in the State, starting the movement and acting as secretary of the general committee which put it over.

I began to write in 1910. Unlike many well known writers, I have had rejections since. At the same time I've found a lot of editors who liked my work. I have written as an avocation ever since. At present I am associate editor for Utah on the staff of *California and Western Medicine,* and the staff of the *Archives of Physical Therapy X-Ray and Radium.* Because of the latter fact I am a member of the American Medical Editors Association.

J.U. Giesy

I am also a member of the Salt Lake Chamber of Commerce, and a life member of the American College of Physical Therapy, which I have served as an officer for several years. My ancestors made me a Son of the American Revolution, and I have made myself more or less of a nuisance to a lot of people all by myself.

I was married in San Francisco, to Juliet Galena Conwell, in December, 1904, and the marriage took. Personally I think they did better work along those lines, that long ago. Anyway we're still living in the same apartment, with no intentions of divorce.

Just why the editor should want to print this confession I really can't imagine. But that's his business. He's asked for it and here it is!

ABOUT THE AUTHOR:
JUNIUS B. SMITH

I WAS BORN at Salt Lake City, Utah, September 29, 1883, at approximately 3:55:27 P.M., right ascension of the mid-heaven (for the benefit of my astrological readers) 16 hrs. 27 min. 57 sec., or 246° 59' 15"; position of planets, Neptune 20° 45' ret. Taurus, Saturn 10° 6' ret. Gemini, Mars 22° 10' Cancer, Jupiter 0° 26' Leo, Moon 22° 24' Virgo, Uranus 24° 34' Virgo, Sun 6° 27' 23" Libra, Venus 8° 52' Libra, Mercury 20° 31' ret. Libra. Declinations: Sun 2° 34' south, Moon 0° 7' south, Neptune 16° 13' north, Uranus 2° 50' north, Saturn 20° 2' north, Jupiter 20° 18' north, Mars 22° 25' north, Venus 2° 20' south, Mercury 11° 17' south.

With this meager astronomical data, the astrologians will know more about me than I could write in a volume.

For the benefit of you other readers:

I am an attorney at law and practiced for many years, paying my office expenses in the lean years by writing. I never had the bitter experience of having to write years before anything sold. At the beginning of my writing career, Dr. J.U. Giesy and I joined intellectual forces, and our first joint effort was submitted to *Argosy* way back in 1911. It sold, first time out. Rapidly we "dashed" off more and they sold also. We each write separately as well as jointly, at such times as we cannot get together.

Early in life I took up astrology as a hobby and lived to see it recognized in judicial decisions as a science. That I have helped, in some measure, to brush away the misconceptions in the minds of many people regarding this much maligned subject is perhaps testified to by my election to Fellowship in the American Academy of Astrologians, an organization that one can't get into for the asking.

Junius B. Smith

I've wasted enough time playing checkers to have built one of the Egyptian pyramids single-handed. Another hobby is shorthand, which has fascinated me for thirty years. I understand several systems. I can sling a wicked toe on the dance floor, but only dance when my weight crowds two hundred. One year I spent the summer on the desert drying out, where my own cooking, plus the heat, effected a material reduction. But I come honestly by it: my father weighed two hundred and sixty in athletic condition—three hundred when not.

And speaking of ancestors: My grandfather was a brother of Joseph Smith, who founded the Mormon Church, which probably explains why I was born in Utah.

THE ARGOSY LIBRARY™

SERIES 4 INCLUDES:

* TUTTLE * ENGLAND * FARLEY *

* BRAND * BRENT * ROSCOE *

* GIESY & SMITH *

* RUD * PETTEE *

* CUNNINGHAM *

THE BEST FICTION
FROM THE FRANK
A. MUNSEY LINE

www.ingramcontent.com/pod-product-compliance
Lightning Source LLC
Chambersburg PA
CBHW030529020726
47494CB00004B/1274